DOCTOR'S DECISION

When ship's doctor Cara Stanford meets trauma consultant Greg Harding, the attraction is immediate — but Greg is battling ghosts from the past and Cara has a new job waiting for her back home in Australia. When the Princess Helena runs into trouble at sea, Greg is winched aboard to help with the casualties, one of whom is Cara. He takes care of her as she recuperates but, thinking there is no future for them, Cara returns to Australia — alone . . .

TERESA ASHBY

DOCTOR'S DECISION

Complete and Unabridged

LINFORD
Leicester

First published in Great Britain

First Linford Edition
published 2013

A catalogue record for this book is available
from the British Library.

ISBN 978–1–4448–1754–6

Published by
F. A. Thorpe (Publishing)
Anstey, Leicestershire
Set by Words & Graphics Ltd.
Anstey, Leicestershire
Printed and bound in Great Britain by
T. J. International Ltd., Padstow, Cornwall

This book is printed on acid-free paper

1

The guard on the port security gate leaned out of his box and as soon as he saw who was driving the silver BMW, his face broke into a huge, welcoming grin.

'Good morning, Dr Harding,' he called out cheerfully as he raised the barrier. 'You're bright and early this morning.'

'Morning, Harry,' Greg called back, surprising the security man with the immediate use of his name. Greg had a good memory for faces and Harry's smile was one he'd never forget. 'How is Chloe now?'

Harry's smile grew wider.

'You remember us,' he said, astounded. 'Well, she's doing great thanks to you. She's just joined a pony club and goes riding twice a week. It's costing me a small fortune, but, well

1

— I'd give her the moon and the stars, you know that.'

'Yes, indeed I do,' Greg said. And he did — on more than one level. There was a certain little boy Greg would give his life for, and he knew just how deep and powerful the love for a child could be. 'I'm glad to hear she's doing well. And she's had no problems from her injuries?'

'None at all,' Harry declared. 'You worked miracles on our girl that day. When I saw her . . . ' He shook his head, his eyes filling at the memory. 'Well, I thought we'd lost her, but you gave her back to us.'

Greg knew how it felt to have memories like that. Haunting memories. If Harry had lost his little girl that day, it would have destroyed him.

'Just pleased to hear she's doing so well,' he said with a grin. 'I'm not surprised about the pony club. She's crazy about horses, isn't she?'

'Sure is,' Harry agreed. 'Why don't you come along and see her in the saddle? You'd think she'd been riding all her life. She loves it. They're putting on a bit of a show and it would be great if you could come and see how well she's doing.'

Greg hesitated and Harry looked embarrassed.

'Sorry,' he said. 'I shouldn't have put you on the spot. You're a very busy man. It was wrong of me to ask. Jumping in with both feet as usual, as my wife would say.'

'I'm delighted you asked,' Greg said. 'I'd love to come. Just tell me when and where and I'll do my best to be there.'

Harry scribbled down an address and time on a piece of paper and handed it over. Greg thanked him and put it in his pocket. He didn't often get the chance to see recovered patients, and he had a lot of time off to take. If there was any way of getting to the stables to see Chloe ride, he'd be there.

He drove through the open barrier, made his way to the staff car park, displayed his permit and pinned his identity badge to his jacket. He was still smiling as he got out of the car.

There were some patients you just never forgot and plucky little Chloe was one of them. Harry's daughter had been crossing the road on a zebra crossing when a motorbike had come from nowhere, hurling her up in the air like a rag doll.

Five years old with multiple fractures, and yet she'd made so little fuss. The resilience and courage of kids never failed to astound him.

Greg had attended at the scene, and at first it had looked as if there was no hope for the small crushed child. But then her eyes had flickered and she'd looked at him and whispered, 'I suppose I won't be able to go to Michaela's party tonight now.'

She'd sounded so cross, so put out, that he'd smiled, knowing right then and there that she was going to make it. It was a memory that never failed to warm him, even now because that little girl had made him smile, something he hadn't done in all those, awful weeks after his brother's death.

Even now, more than two years later, not a day passed when something didn't make him think of Brad, and the memories were always painful. He wondered what Harry would make of it if he told him the truth — that little Chloe had brought him back from the brink in a way; had shaken him from his helpless, hopeless despair.

And then of course along came that other special child, little Danny, whom Greg had immediately taken to his heart.

He'd been present at Danny's birth and had been first to hold him when the baby's mother had turned her head away and begged them to take him from her. Thankfully her rejection hadn't lasted long and within a few hours, she was holding Danny to her breast, gazing down at him with wonder.

But those few hours when all Danny had was Greg had left their mark, made him aware of the enormity of his responsibility to his brother's widow and child.

The pain and guilt over Brad's death would never go away, but he'd learned to live with it.

* * *

He was far too early for the meeting and rather than make his way to the stuffy confines of the boardroom, he walked out onto the quayside. Just the sight and sound of the waves gently lapping against the harbour edge made him feel cool, and there was a brisk breeze chopping up the sea which helped drop the temperature of this hot, late summer day.

Almost everyone he passed called out a greeting. Most people knew him, either from the hospital or through his work at the port.

The dock was a hive of activity. Towering cranes worked constantly, lorries poured off a cargo ship in one of the far berths and tractor units charged up and down, transporting containers from the dock to the storage area. Several freighters were lined up in the berths, but the ship that caught his eye was the Princess Helena.

Small, elegant, a bunting-laden jewel tagged on to the end of a line of ungainly cargo vessels, she was a much more compact cruise ship than most of the huge liners that docked here.

She looked like a refined, elegant lady amongst a crowd of burly navvies.

He took off his jacket and slung it over his shoulder as he strolled along the dockside, then he paused and looked over the side at the water which was as dark and as green as his eyes. What he wouldn't give to throw off his clothes and dive into that deep, cool water.

It was quieter at this end of the dock by the empty berths and he felt the need for solitude ahead of what promised to be a difficult meeting. There was no one else about, apart from a few dockers enjoying a break well away from the hustle and bustle elsewhere.

He needed a few quiet minutes to get his thoughts together and think about what he was going to say.

The wind had ruffled his dark hair, but a flick with a comb would soon remedy that and he was enjoying the feeling of exhilaration and freedom that being this close to the sea always brought. Further down the dock, he heard the sound of cheering and whistling and turned to face the wind to see the distant, approaching figure of a woman jogging past the resting dockers.

Nothing unusual in that — except this wasn't really the place you expected to see joggers. It was a highly irresponsible thing to be doing, even if she was keeping to the quiet end. Ports were busy, hazardous places at the best of times.

He really felt he should step out in her path and point out the dangers, but even as the thought crossed his mind he could almost hear his late brother chuckling in his ear.

Get over yourself, Greg. She's not doing any harm to herself or anyone else. Stop being so stuffy.

'Stuffy?' he whispered aloud and he nearly smiled.

* ★ ★

Cara Sanford checked her watch as her feet pounded along the dockside. Hot and breathless, she knew this was her last chance to run on solid ground for some time. For the next two weeks, she would have to make do with a jog around the decks of the Princess Helena. Her short blonde hair bounced as she ran, but around her face, it clung damply to her flushed skin.

To the left of her, a group of dockers taking a break called out to her. Someone wolf-whistled. Cara acknowledged it as a compliment with a cheery wave, but didn't break her stride.

As she drew closer to the cruise ship, she spotted a man standing by the water's edge and her pace slowed a little. He looked out of place somehow. The briefcase, she thought with a grin, was completely wrong here. She couldn't help but look at him as she approached. Tall, dark-haired and slim, but with wide shoulders. He wore a crisp white shirt and black trousers and stood with his jacket casually slung over one shoulder.

He was watching her as she got closer and she realised he was frowning. Oh, don't say he was some sort of port official about to give her a ticking-off for running along the quay . . .

He kept looking at her steadily, while remaining still and calm. Maybe he was a member of the crew of the Princess Helena — someone she'd be working alongside over the course of the next fortnight.

An entertainer, perhaps? Yes, she could see him on stage, singing, and he had the kind of looks that would turn knees to jelly and make hearts beat faster.

Not hers, though. She was immune to men like that. All men, in fact. There was definitely no room in Cara Sanford's life for romance and relationships. Perhaps he was one of the nurses — now that would be a turn up for the books.

Well, whoever he was, she wished she wasn't quite so hot and sweaty. It was hardly the best first impression.

He was smiling now, she could see. A rather lop-sided smile in a strong, rugged face. His hair was dark, almost black, and what hadn't been blown about by the wind curled against his strong tanned neck. All this she noticed in the brief seconds of her approach as she unconsciously slowed her pace even more.

'Hi,' she called breathlessly as she passed and she crossed her fingers because she didn't want him to tell her off because then she'd be forced to give him a piece of her mind. She hated getting off on the wrong foot with people.

'Hello,' he replied, his voice as deep and dark as his eyes, and for a moment it seemed to her that he might have added something else, but he simply took a step back to let her go by.

Phew, thank goodness for that, Cara thought as she passed.

* * *

Greg felt torn. He ought to stop the young woman right away for her own safety.

One thing he knew was that he'd never seen her before. He was sure he would have remembered, but there was nothing familiar about her — from her short, shaggy blonde hair clinging around her perfectly heart-shaped face, to her long tanned legs. She wore a pair of white shorts that hugged her curves and a lemon vest top darkened with sweat. She wasn't the young girl he'd first thought, but someone nearer his own age.

Old enough to know better, he thought to himself.

She smiled warmly as she greeted him and the reprimand died in his throat.

After he'd said hello, he turned away and watched the sea, keeping his eyes on a passing tugboat and the mewling gulls skimming the water. Sure, she was attractive, a nice-looking woman, but he wasn't interested.

But then she cried out, and he wheeled round and saw her falling to the ground. The doctor in him took over, overriding everything else as the reasons for her going down began to crowd in his head. And he was already running towards her, dropping his jacket and his briefcase as he ran.

'Argh, I feel such an idiot,' she blurted as he approached, her Australian accent noticeable but faint.

'This really isn't the place for running,' he said and hated the pompous sound of his own voice. That would really have made Brad laugh. Greg had always been the more serious of the brothers.

Brad would have come out with some witty line and made her laugh. Greg had simply made her scowl. His brother had got all the charm as well as the lion's share of the recklessness . . .

'You don't say,' she said dryly.

'Actually, I do say. A working port is a dangerous place for this kind of casual activity, as you have found to your cost. There are vehicles rushing up and down, men trying to work, cranes . . . '

'Yes, I get the picture,' she retorted. 'I had noticed my surroundings. And believe it or not, I was being careful.'

She had a graze on her forearm, but seemed more concerned with her ankle.

'Let me,' he said.

'No, it's fine,' she said and tried to pull her ankle away.

'I'm a doctor,' they both said in unison and were taken aback as much by the coincidence as by the irritated tone they had both adopted to make the statement.

They stared at each other in amazement, then both laughed — and she had the most wonderful, warm laugh. Her eyes were so blue. Greg had never seen such clear eyes in such a beautiful colour. As blue as a Wedgwood plate and ringed with the thickest, darkest lashes he'd ever seen. Her pupils grew huge, almost obliterating the blue with their darkness as she looked up at him.

Not that it meant anything to him, he told himself.

Their mutual laughter did the job of breaking the ice and Greg felt himself relax.

'It's just twisted,' she insisted. 'Not even sprained. I guess I was lucky. It doesn't even hurt very much. I think the battered pride is probably the worst of my injuries. I feel such an idiot!'

'It won't hurt to let me take a look,' he said, but she was right, there was no swelling there, no sign of damage. She was fit, well-muscled, her skin smooth.

His fingers gently massaged and probed her ankle until he was satisfied she was telling him the truth.

'I told you it was fine. I'm ship's doctor on the Helena,' she said. 'How about you?'

'Orthopaedic and Trauma Consultant at the local hospital,' he responded.

'Snap,' she said. 'Well, sort of. When I get home, I'm taking up a post as Director of Emergency Services. I daresay it boils down to the same thing.'

'Home? Australia?' He wondered what had brought her all the way over to England.

'Yes,' she answered, and suddenly home felt so much further away than it already was. 'So what are you doing here?'

He helped her to her feet, and she leaned against him while testing her weight on the ankle.

His arm slid naturally round her slim waist and he could feel the heat of her skin through her thin clothes.

'Try putting some weight on it. Easy now.'

'There, that's fine,' she said. 'You can let go of me now. I promise I won't collapse in a heap. And you haven't said what you're doing here.'

She looked up at him, waiting for an answer as she stood perfectly well on her own two feet.

'I'm here for a meeting,' he said briskly. 'Every year we have a major emergency exercise. We just need to discuss the finer points and settle on a date to suit all parties.'

'I guess that explains your rather over-officious attitude,' she teased.

'Officious attitude?' he repeated, offended. 'You seriously think that what you were doing was okay? Apart from the danger aspect, you're putting the men off their work. You could cause an accident.'

'Oh, don't be ridiculous,' she retorted and he looked so taken aback, she softened her tone. 'I was joking! You need to lighten up. Look, I understand your concerns, but trust me, I really do know what I'm doing. So tell me, what does this emergency exercise involve? I'd guess it doesn't include mad women jogging along the docks.'

He was about to snap back at her, but her question was a genuine one and it was a subject about which he was passionate. He wasn't used to her kind of teasing, either. People usually took him very seriously.

'We have volunteers from the port to act as casualties. They get a paid day off work. Everyone seems to see it as a bit of fun. The way some of the casualties ham it up, you'd think they were budding thespians.'

'I hope it all goes well,' she said.

'I'm sure it will,' he replied.

'As long as no more lunatics mess up the dock by falling over,' she added with a smile.

'I'm sure they won't.' His smile wasn't altogether reluctant.

'Well,' she said. 'It was nice meeting you, Doctor . . . ?'

'Harding,' he answered. 'And it's Greg.'

'Cara Sanford,' she responded. 'Cara.'

He wanted to see her walk on that ankle, make sure it didn't give out on her and send her crashing to the ground again.

'Was there something else?'

'You sure that ankle is okay?' he asked.

'Sure,' she said, hopping from one foot to the other. 'See.'

He took a deep breath. 'I'd better — '

'Me too,' she said.

'You'll be all right?'

She nodded.

'Goodbye then. Enjoy your cruise. And good luck in your new job, Cara.'

'Thanks,' she said, standing still as he backed away. 'Good luck with your meeting.'

'And no more jogging along the docks,' he added sternly. He tried to make it sound like a joke, but it came out sounding all formal and censorious.

At last he turned, stooped to pick up

his jacket and briefcase from the ground and brushed off the dust. Time to get to work!

★ ★ ★

Cara watched until he'd gone around the side of the main port building and disappeared from view. Now there was a handsome guy, or he would be if he wasn't quite so starchy. And he was so tall! Cara was quite tall herself and it was unusual for her to look up quite so far at another person. And she'd never seen such green eyes before in her life. They were very unusual. The irises were ringed with a circle of black, and flecked with gold — and she was most disturbed to discover she'd noticed so much during such a brief exchange.

She'd even noticed the small dimple in his chin, but who wouldn't? It was quite a feature.

But honestly, what was the guy thinking, talking to her as if she were some kind of fool?

Of course, you weren't supposed to be able to tell what a person was like at first glance. Yet she could see he had presence, dignity and passion. Oh, the passion was perhaps the strongest impression of all, as if underneath that cool, crisp exterior, he was simmering with it.

Then again, he did seem rather full of his own self-importance. Some doctors were like that. Thought they were God's gift to mankind in general, and women in particular.

Just like Dad. So beautiful, so charming and so treacherous.

Poor Mum. Fell in love with Dad, gave up everything for him — and for what? To be pushed into the shadows until she turned into a shadow herself. A shadow that ate and breathed but didn't know how to live any more. And then, ultimately, she was unceremoniously dumped for a younger model. It was possible to die of a broken heart; Cara had seen it happen to her mother.

Tread carefully, Cara, she imagined

her mother whispering in her ear. *Don't lose your head after all these years. Be strong.*

'Do I look stupid?' Cara answered herself softly. And then she realised that she could hear voices, real voices, not imagined ones.

She became aware that she was surrounded by people and had been standing lost in thought for far too long. A band, made up of young musicians from a local school, were setting themselves up to play the passengers aboard. Supplies were being loaded onto the ship from huge lorries she had failed to notice arrive, and a group of young men stood nearby wearing yellow hard hats and luminous waistcoats.

Cara felt a tear trickle down her cheek. It still hurt, even now, to think about her mother. They'd been so close, but during those last few agonising months, Cara hadn't been able to reach her. If only she'd done more, perhaps things would have turned out differently.

For goodness' sake, girl, get a grip. Cara Sanford doesn't cry. She hasn't cried for years and this wet on my face is just the wind blowing grit in my eyes.

She moved towards the young men as she made her way back to the ship. Not one of them looked more than eighteen years old. Cara pasted on a smile. She'd found through the years that a smile, however forced it might be to begin with, soon turned into something real. And it was much nicer to smile than to frown.

'Hi,' she said cheerfully. 'Are you the baggage handlers?'

'That's right. You're Australian,' one of them said.

She looked at his name badge.

'Yes, I am, Simon,' she said. Looking at these fresh-faced young guys she couldn't believe any of them did this for a living. 'I guess this isn't a full-time job for any of you?'

'We're all doing A-levels,' Simon explained. He seemed a little more confident than the others and she guessed he was their team leader. He had the kind of authority that would stand him in good stead as he got older. 'We just come to work as and when we're required.'

'It's the middle of the night sometimes,' another boy chipped in. Mark, according to his badge.

'Really,' Cara said. 'That must be tough.'

'It is on my mum,' someone else piped up. 'She has to drive me down here.'

They all laughed and began to recount tales of doting parents making sure they had breakfast and driving them down to the port in the small hours. Cara stood chatting with them for a few minutes, enjoying their youthful banter. And it was strange how apparently independent and grown-up young men still seemed to depend so much on their mothers.

Cara couldn't remember a time that she'd depended on her mother for anything. In their relationship, it was the other way round. Cara had grown up knowing that the only person she could ever rely on was herself.

'When are you expecting the first passengers to arrive?'

'Any time now,' Simon told her. 'The first coaches are due, then the boat train will arrive and there are a few who come by car and taxi. Then it'll be all go until everything is loaded.'

'So what happens? You carry the luggage aboard piece by piece?' Cara asked.

They all laughed again and she couldn't help smiling, enjoying their youthful exuberance. She needed this. Needed to be lifted out of the darkness that had temporarily enveloped her.

'We load it onto crates — called brutes,' Simon explained. 'On the bigger ships, the brutes are loaded straight into the side of the vessel, but on small ones like the Helena, they're craned onto the deck.'

'But first, it all has to go through

X-ray,' Mark said. 'Just in case anyone's trying to bring anything dodgy aboard.'

'Well, it's been nice meeting you all,' Cara said, looking at her watch. 'If the first passengers are due, I'd better get on board and get ready.'

'Are you one of the entertainers?' someone asked.

'I bet you're the fitness expert,' another voice guessed. Then suddenly they were all guessing, everything from a singer to head chef.

'Actually, you're all wrong,' she answered, smiling. 'I'm the ship's doctor.'

'No way,' Simon said. 'I mean, you don't look like a doctor.'

She laughed and wondered what they thought a doctor should look like.

'Well, I'm not sure whether I should take that as a compliment or not,' she retorted.

'Oh, it's a compliment,' Simon assured her. 'If I were ill I'd rather see you than some boring old man.'

Cara thought briefly of Greg Harding and laughed.

'Not all doctors are boring old men,' she returned. 'Anyway, there's a lot to be said for age and experience. But I really must be on my way.'

'Enjoy your trip,' Simon said and the others called out goodbye, one of the boys lifting his hard hat as she departed. She found that simple gesture rather sweet and touching, and the smile on her face as she walked away didn't have to be forced at all.

* * *

Walking into the boardroom was like stepping into an oven and Greg recoiled a little as the hot, stale air blasted him full in the face.

'Oh, it's hot in here,' remarked George Hammond, the fire chief, as he followed Greg into the large meeting room.

Greg turned, surprised to see him here. George had been involved in a pretty bad accident not long ago, but he'd told Greg he'd be back — if only behind a desk.

'Well, until the port invests in air conditioning, we'll have these windows open,' Greg said. 'It's a shame to be portside and not take advantage of the sea breeze.'

'Hear, hear,' George agreed. 'And since it promises to be a long meeting, we may as well make ourselves comfortable.'

George moved to help Greg open the windows and received a stern look.

'You shouldn't be reaching up like that,' he said. 'You were told to take things easy after the accident.'

George chuckled. 'Don't you ever stop being a doctor, Greg?'

'It's in my blood,' Greg answered. 'Now sit down and leave the windows to me, or I'll tell Stella.'

'Ouch,' George said as he sat down. 'You really know how to scare a guy, don't you?'

'Good thing too,' Greg remarked. George's wife, five foot tall Stella, was a force to be reckoned with. 'I don't want to see you rushed back into my department on a trolley because you won't follow doctor's orders.'

'And I thought I was one of your favourite patients.'

'Oh, you are, George,' Greg said. 'And one of my prettiest.'

'Stop flirting, you two,' Ted, the chief dock foreman, shouted across the room and everyone laughed. Greg and George were two of the most masculine-looking men present.

They held these meetings once a year to discuss the annual major incident exercise which involved all the emergency services and the local hospitals. The County was the largest of the hospitals in the area, and the one that would take the bulk of any casualties.

As Greg pushed open the windows, a brisk breeze swept in, ruffling the papers on the table, but it was air and it was fresh even if it was warm.

The boardroom was on the second floor of the main port building and it

looked out over the cruise ship berths
— and more specifically, the Princess
Helena.

And there was Cara, still on the dock,
surrounded by a group of young
baggage handlers. They were all laughing and he felt a prickle of irritation.
This was a busy working port with huge
lumps of machinery moving about. It
wasn't the place for casual meetings.
Hadn't she heard a word he'd said?

'Crew? One of the dancers?' George
asked and Greg realised the fire chief
was back on his feet and had been
watching her too.

'Ship's doctor, I believe,' he replied
nonchalantly.

'Nice looker,' George said with a
grin.

'Really?' Greg said coolly. 'I hadn't
noticed.'

'And you just happened to know she
was ship's doctor?' George went on
with a twinkle in his eye. 'Come on,
Greg. Don't look at me like that. I
didn't come down in the last shower.'

The fire chief's face softened and he squeezed Greg's shoulder. The laughter left his eyes and he became serious.

'What happened, happened, Greg,' he said. 'I was there, remember? It was just one of those awful freaky things and there was nothing any of us could do about it. I lost some good men that night, too. Sons, husbands, fathers. But life goes on. You can't punish yourself for the rest of your life for something that wasn't your fault.'

Greg stared at the older man. He felt as if he'd been stripped and all his emotions and feelings were laid bare. If anyone else had spoken to him like that, scratched at the place where he was still raw, he'd have decked them on the spot.

'You know your trouble, George?' he said tersely. 'You've been listening in on too many of these counselling sessions.'

In his pocket, Greg's mobile phone began to ring. He was glad of the excuse to end this conversation.

'Excuse me a minute,' he said.

He left the room to answer the call.

'Greg? It's me, Claire.' His sister-in-law's voice sounded strained, as it usually did.

'What is it?' Greg asked. 'Is everything all right, Claire?'

'Could you drop in and see Danny?' she asked. 'I'm worried about him. He's a bit under the weather.'

'Sure,' Greg said. 'What's the problem?'

'He's just a bit miserable and out of sorts. You know how he gets sometimes,' she said.

Yes, Greg knew exactly how he got. The poor kid was probably going stir crazy having spent yet another sunny day stuck at home. But how could he blame Claire for that? He suspected that she was just as lonely and fed-up as Danny and that she wanted him to call in as much to see her as his nephew.

'Sorry if I disturbed you,' she said. 'Is it today you've got your meeting at the port?'

'I'm here now,' he said. 'The meeting

is about to start.'

'Oh, Greg, I'm sorry,' she gasped. 'I wouldn't have called if I'd known.'

'No problem,' he assured her. 'You know you can call me any time. You could bring Danny down if you like, later, and I'll arrange a tour of the dock for you both. He could watch the cruise ship sail. He'd like that.'

Even as he asked, he knew the refusal would be forming on her lips. It was a battle to get Claire to leave the house at all, and if it weren't for him, Danny would never go anywhere either.

It seemed Claire was the one person he couldn't patch up and put right. And because of it, Danny was suffering. Claire was a loving mother who took good care of her son, but he needed to spread his wings and she kept them closely clipped.

He wound up the call and returned to the boardroom. He meant what he said about Claire contacting him any time. He'd made a promise to himself that he would always care for his brother's wife and child and it was a promise he took seriously because maybe, just maybe, if he'd done things differently, Brad would have been around to take care of them himself.

Who was he kidding? There was no maybe about it. It was his fault Brad was dead.

More people began to arrive. Representatives from two police forces, paramedics and fire officers as well as port staff filed into the room. Greg allowed himself one final look at Cara who was now hurrying towards the crew's gangplank, then with a wistful breath, took his place at the table ready for the conference to begin.

2

Up on deck, Cara placed her hands on the rail and looked down along the dock. She liked her freedom, freedom to run when and where she wanted, and although she'd only been on the ship for a few hours, she had felt oddly constrained and had a powerful urge to get back on terra firma. Her cabin was small and, being in the centre of the ship next to the medical centre, had no porthole.

At the same time she wished she hadn't bothered going for a run, or had confined herself to running round the deck. She hadn't enjoyed her run-in with Greg Harding. It had left her feeling unsettled, but she didn't know why.

'I was told I'd find you here,' a voice said and she turned to see a slight man with neat grey hair and an even neater grey beard approaching her, his hand extended. 'Ray Harrison. I'm your nurse. You are Dr Sanford?'

'Cara,' she said. 'Yes, that's me. It's good to meet you, Ray. Have you had a tour of the ship and acquainted yourself with the medical centre?'

'No need,' Ray explained. 'I'm a regular on the Helena. Lucy, the other cruise nurse, is going to join the ship when we stop at La Coruna. The chances of us needing two nurses before then are almost non-existent.'

'Careful!' Cara laughed. 'That sounds very much like famous last words to me. It's never a good idea to tempt fate.'

'I wouldn't have marked you down as the superstitious kind.'

'I'm not,' she said, but there was an unmistakable shiver down her spine.

He joined her at the rail and leaned on it beside her.

'I see the uniforms are gathering for their annual fun and games,' he observed, nodding towards the main port building.

'Ah, the major incident exercise,' Cara said. 'Greg Harding was telling me about it.'

'You've met Greg, then,' Ray commented. 'Nice bloke, very good doctor. Shame about the baggage he insists on carrying round. Have you ever done anything like this before, Cara?'

Cara hesitated. She was tempted to ask Ray about Greg. But to what end? It was unlikely they would ever meet again. Besides, to ask Ray what he meant would be perilously close to gossip and Cara had never gone in for gossip.

'First time,' she said cheerily.

'Think you'll make it a regular thing or are you reserving judgement? It's not for everyone, and for the most part it can be pretty boring. The only excitement we're likely to get for the next fortnight is the lifeboat drill we'll do before we leave port.'

'There you go again. Tempting fate!

37

I'll be quite happy if we do have a quiet, uneventful trip. I've got a new job waiting for me at home which is going to be challenging enough,' she explained. 'So this will be my first and last stint on board. It's a kind of working holiday.'

'Nervous?'

She smiled slowly. Somehow people didn't usually expect doctors to be nervous, in possession of normal human feelings.

'A little,' she admitted. 'It's a bit of a step into the unknown. Is it that obvious? I don't want to scare my patients.'

'Not at all. It's just I remember my first time. I was as nervous as hell. Worrying about being seasick and not being able to do my job properly.'

Cara hooted with laughter. 'That is exactly what worries me,' she admitted. 'I'm glad to know it's a common fear.'

'You'll be fine,' Ray assured her. 'If you're busy, you forget about being seasick and if you're not busy, well it doesn't really matter, does it?'

'I guess not. Thanks, Ray.'

'You're welcome. I'm looking forward to working with you, Cara,' Ray said with a grin. 'I'll either be in the medical centre or my cabin if you want me. I'm going to have a shower, then get into uniform.'

★   ★   ★

The meeting could have been going better. It had started with the operations manager, Ralph Carter, getting to his feet and announcing that this year's exercise would involve a fire on ship.

When he'd finished, he sat down and Greg rose. He'd been biding his time, waiting for Carter to finish. With his patients, Greg had endless reserves of patience, but with people like Carter, his fuse was already very short and getting shorter all the time.

'A fire on board ship. Didn't we do that two years ago?' he began slowly. 'Terrible as it would be, it is not a major incident. We need to stretch our resources to the limit, because if there is ever a major incident, then believe me, we are going to be stretched. And the whole point of all of this is to see if and how we cope as a team.'

Carter played with a pen, turning it end to end through his fingers as if he wasn't really listening. He probably wasn't. He was the type to make up his mind and expect everyone else to fall in with him.

Greg looked around, knowing he had the support of most of the people there, even if no one else was willing to stand up and be counted.

'It may inconvenience you to do it my way, but in the event of a real emergency, it could save lives.'

'Have you finished, Dr Harding?' Carter asked.

'I haven't even started yet,' Greg shot back and George Hammond gave him a wry grin. 'Every year I raise this point and every year you dismiss my proposals,' Greg continued, his frustration visible. 'What is the point of us having a set scenario for these major incident exercises?'

He glanced at Ted, the chief dock foreman, who gave him a small nod of support.

'Try to keep hold of that famous temper of yours, Doctor,' Carter said dryly.

'Temper? Oh, believe me, I'm a long way from losing my temper,' Greg returned.

'But you don't seem to understand the logistics. As long as we know what we're dealing with, we can prepare for it,' Carter said. 'We need to be able to make plans, to be able to ensure we have enough volunteer casualties and enough time to carry out the exercise without disrupting port operations.'

Greg moved from the table to the window and looked out.

There was no sign of Cara. He wondered why, in the heat of this exchange, he'd even noticed.

He turned slowly from the window.

'That is my point exactly,' he said passionately, because this was a subject he felt passionate about and it was Carter's problem if he decided to take passion for anger. 'Let's say a terrorist turns up in a boat and rams into the side of the Princess Helena down there. Only she's fully loaded with passengers and they're about to sail off into the sunset. The ship is holed, fire breaks out, there's mass panic on board. One of the tractor units gets a piece of blazing wreckage hurled at it and unable to see where he's going, the driver swerves and rams into that little band of kids down there.'

He looked round. He'd got everyone's attention now.

'The band is mostly made up of kids from the local schools,' he went on, driving his point home. 'So you've got a burning ship and you've got to evacuate injured and frightened passengers. Not only that, the ship is sinking and the flames are threatening that dangerous cargo you've got on that freighter in number four berth. Meanwhile the tractor unit, having ploughed through the kids, has gone over the side and you've got a man trapped under water in his vehicle. What are you going to do?'

There was a moment of silence, then Carter answered, 'It wouldn't happen, Greg.'

Greg groaned aloud, and he wasn't the only one in the room to do so. There was no getting through to some people. Carter didn't seem to understand that anything *could* happen — and when and if it did, the emergency services would be stretched to the limit. Surely it was better to push that limit in an exercise so that they'd know they could rely on well co-ordinated teamwork in any eventuality?

'We need to know how to handle a real crisis,' Greg continued, desperation giving his voice an edge. 'We do a fire one year, a chemical spill the next, but in real life these kinds of emergencies don't follow a script and neither should we. As a professional, I'd prefer to handle an unknown scenario. I know we can cope at the hospital, but it's the on-the-scene casualties I'm worried about. Getting the police, fire service and medics to work together.'

Carter smiled.

'I do understand,' he said. 'But as I say, port operations . . . '

'In the event of the sort of major emergency that could happen here, you may not have a port to worry about,' Greg returned softly.

He looked round the room.

'As it happens, I agree with Dr Harding,' George Hammond said, getting to his feet. 'It would be more of a challenge and give us a better indication of how we would cope in a genuine emergency as a team if the whole thing were to be sprung on us as a surprise.'

'George?' Carter said, his voice heavy with implication. 'I didn't see you there. Should you be here? Are you fully recovered? Perhaps you'd like a glass of water.'

Greg didn't like the sneer in Carter's voice. He liked even less the fact that it was directed at a close friend.

'It was the chief's body that was damaged in the accident, not his ability to think,' Greg said. 'George has always been, and remains, a crucial member of this team.'

'I agree,' the doctor representing the nearby GP unit said. 'You could say George is the linchpin of this whole enterprise. As for Greg's proposal, well, I'm all for it. Obviously we would have to know the time and date, but that's all we need to know.'

One by one, other voices spoke up in support of Greg. He could see the other side's point of view, but just for once he'd like to see how they'd work under real pressure.

'Let's adjourn for refreshments,' Carter said smoothly as the meeting looked set to become as heated as the day outside. 'Please, help yourselves from the buffet table. We'll reconvene in an hour's time.'

Greg had no appetite. He returned once again to the window and saw a loaded brute being towed towards the Princess Helena. A handful of the boys were on the deck of the ship waiting for the brute to be craned aboard.

The first of the coaches must have arrived.

'I'm going out for some air,' he said abruptly to George, and left the room.

★ ★ ★

Cara chose a pair of loose-fitting cream trousers and a sleeveless white shirt to wear for greeting the passengers. She'd showered, washed her hair and put on some make-up and now felt ready to face the world.

There was a knock on her door and she opened it with a smile which quickly faded when she saw the look on the young steward's face.

'Come quick, Doctor,' he said.

'There's been an accident!'

'What kind of accident?'

'One of the brutes,' he explained. 'The side hadn't been properly secured. The full load dropped onto the deck.'

'Injuries?'

'Someone's badly hurt. They've put him on a sun bed, but . . . '

'They moved him?' Cara gasped, horrified.

Cara raced through to the medical centre, grabbed her bag, told the steward to find Ray and bring a trolley, then took off at a run along the corridors. Thank goodness they hadn't started to board the passengers yet, and those that had arrived were in the arrivals lounge on the quay unaware of the drama on board ship. The lifts would be too slow and she'd never been one to walk when she could run, so she sprinted up the stairs.

Her thoughts were with the casualty. How badly was he hurt? God forbid the brute had fallen on him. Those things were so big and heavy — and falling from a height, oh dear Lord.

No point thinking ahead at this stage. She had to be ready to deal with whatever faced her when she arrived on scene.

She burst through the doors onto the deck and took in the scene at a glance. The brute lay on the deck, its contents spilled far and wide and as if they sensed her arrival, the group of youngsters moved aside as she approached.

'If you're all okay, I suggest you move well away,' she told them and when they just stood there, she added gently, 'It's okay, I've got him now.'

Then she looked at the boy stretched out on the sun bed.

'Simon,' she murmured. Oh, why did it have to be him? Why did it have to be any of this band of young men?

* * *

Cara could see why they'd moved him. The deck was littered with clothing and broken glass. Even with the brisk wind blowing, the smell of spilled perfume was overpowering. Kate Benton, the purser, and Andrew Parsons, one of the ship's senior officers, were in attendance. Cara remembered them from her earlier tour of the ship. She'd taken to Kate straight away.

'Anyone else hurt?' she asked. 'And please tell me you've called an ambulance.'

'First thing we did after sending for you,' Kate said. 'We're so glad you're here, Cara.'

'Mostly there are just a few minor scrapes,' Andrew said. 'But this boy seems quite stunned. I saw it happen. He realised the brute was breaking open and pushed the others out of the way, taking the brunt of it himself. He's having trouble breathing. It's probably shock, don't you think?'

Alarm bells clanged.

'It isn't shock,' Cara said. 'Not in the sense you mean.'

'Well, he doesn't appear to have any

injuries,' Andrew said.

Cara knew otherwise, but she wasn't going to waste time getting into an argument.

'All right, Simon?' She smoothed his sweat-drenched curly fair hair back from his face. 'You're going to be okay. I'm going to take care of you now.'

She didn't like the look of him at all. He was perspiring heavily and his skin had a blue tinge. She licked her lips, not liking the direction her thoughts were taking, but knowing she had to go with her instincts. After all, they'd never let her down yet. And she'd seen this before enough times to recognise it for what it was.

He didn't speak. Instead he was putting all his effort into breathing, growling with every breath as his body struggled frantically to keep air in his lungs.

'I don't expect an answer, Simon,' she said, as she pulled her stethoscope from her bag. 'Don't try to speak, my love.'

He closed his eyes in the only gesture of acquiescence he was capable of.

She lifted his shirt and saw straight away what was causing the trouble. As she'd suspected, he had a penetrating wound to his chest. The hole was acting like a valve, allowing air into the chest cavity, but closing with expiration. Something from the brute must have caused the puncture wound.

Ideally it would be best to get Simon to hospital, but he didn't have time. She would have preferred to move him to the medical centre, but that too would take time and it was clear that for Simon, time had almost run out. Quicker to put a chest drain in here and now.

She turned to the steward who had just arrived with a trolley.

'Go back to the medical centre,' she said. 'Find Ray. Tell him I need oxygen and a thoracic pack, pleural drainage system, large bore cannula and . . . '

The young steward looked baffled and frightened. Cara thought again.

She wasn't working in a hospital now where everyone knew exactly what she was talking about. In fact a very frightened audience surrounded her. She had to think like a layman and keep it simple.

'Just tell him to bring everything I'll need for a chest drain, okay?' she amended. 'He'll know what I need. And do it fast,' she added sharply when he just stood staring at her. 'You're wasting time.'

He came to his senses and ran off. She wouldn't normally have been so sharp, especially with someone as frightened as the steward, but she couldn't afford to waste a single second. She turned to Kate.

'Alert the ambulance crew that Simon's injury is life threatening,' she said softly. 'And that speed is of the essence. He has a pneumothorax.'

Cara didn't need X-rays to confirm that Simon had the condition. The volume of air trapped in his pleural cavity was increasing with every painful, ragged breath he took. Breath sounds on the affected side were absent and she knew that before long, his other lung may cease to function and the blood flow to his heart would stop. He could be dead in minutes — or even sooner.

He was tachycardic, his heart racing at over a hundred and forty beats per minute, which added weight to Cara's diagnosis. Ideally she would have preferred to get him to hospital, but time was running away from her like sand in an egg timer.

By the time the steward returned carrying oxygen, Cara had dealt with the wound, sealing the dressing on three sides.

'I couldn't find Ray, but you said you needed oxygen and he gave me this,' he said, his eyes round with fright. 'He said he'll put together everything you need and be here straight away.'

What on earth did he mean? Couldn't find Ray but he'd put together what she needed? She shook her head.

As long as she got the equipment, that was all that mattered.

'Thank you,' she said, smiling because she felt the steward needed the praise after his earlier hesitation and her sharpness with him. She was sorry about that and would apologise later, but right now Simon was her only concern. 'Well done.'

Kate was on her way back.

'How long is the ambulance likely to take?' Cara asked as she slipped the oxygen mask over Simon's face.

'Fifteen minutes at the outside,' Kate replied.

Cara nodded'. Fifteen minutes to get here, then the journey to the hospital — she really had no choice but to proceed.

'Simon, listen to me. Your chest cavity is filling up with air and that's what's making it hard for you to breathe. I'm going to have to put a drain in your chest to let the air out. Do you understand what I'm saying?'

IIe nodded weakly and looked up at

her with frightened eyes. That more than anything got to her — the fear in the eyes of her patients. She could alleviate pain, but fear was far more difficult to deal with.

'Once I've done that, you'll feel instant relief. All right, Simon? It will make breathing easier for you, but it means I'll have to do it now.'

Her attention was so focused on the boy that she didn't notice the quiet arrival of another person.

'Oh, where on earth has Ray got to?' she muttered.

'Will I do?'

She looked up and saw Greg and her heart thumped painfully against her ribs. Would he do? You bet he would. Another doctor on the scene, brilliant.

'Only if you've brought the thoracic pack,' she said.

'I have,' he said. 'I sent the steward ahead with the oxygen while I put everything else you'd need together.'

There was no time to ask where Ray was, Cara was just grateful that at last she could get on with saving Simon's life. She didn't know how or why Greg was here, but she was delighted to see him.

'I'm going to have to do this here and now,' Cara said as she drew Greg to one side. 'I have no choice in the matter. He'll die if I don't.'

'I know,' Greg said and she was grateful to him for not questioning her decision. He didn't even know her, yet he was prepared to trust her judgement. Professionally that meant a great deal.

Greg helped her remove Simon's shirt and sit him up, then beckoned Andrew over to take his place, supporting Simon in a sitting position.

'This isn't a pleasant procedure,' Greg warned him. 'Unless you have a strong stomach, I suggest you don't watch. We need you to hold him steady. If you don't think you're up to it I'd rather you were honest. No one will think any the less of you.'

Andrew swallowed hard and nodded. 'I'll be okay. Just take care of the boy.'

'Okay.' Greg placed his hand on his arm and squeezed lightly. 'But any time you want out, you just yell, okay? I'd rather have some warning if you feel at all unsure.'

'Okay.'

This wasn't the ideal place to be carrying out the procedure, but Cara had no choice. She washed her hands quickly with antiseptic wash, then snapped on gloves. Greg followed suit.

Cara was used to trusting her nurses to know what she'd need for such a procedure and to have everything ready and to hand. She had to trust that Greg would be as reliable and ready as any good emergency nurse and that he'd brought everything she'd need.

While Greg prepared the drainage bottle with sterile water and placed the drainage tube correctly, Cara set to work on Simon. She quickly found the angle of Louis, then counted down until she found the fifth intercostal space.

She didn't have to ask — Greg was

already passing her a pen to mark the site of insertion of the cannula. Swiftly, she cleaned the area.

'Lidocaine?'

'Ready.'

'All right, Simon. Hold in there. You'll feel a little scratch.'

She spoke out of habit. Simon was past caring about scratches, little or otherwise, and was very close to losing consciousness. Greg passed her the syringe and Cara injected Lidocaine into the site where she intended to insert the cannula, feeling a give as the needle pierced the pleura.

'I'm in,' she whispered as she aspirated air into the syringe.

Working with a speed and deftness that astounded Greg, Cara inserted a purse string suture, then made a transverse incision. It was like watching an accomplished artist at work, her long, slender fingers so quick and capable and moving with a fluid rhythm that was almost hypnotic.

'Sinus forceps,' she said and they

were in her hand instantly. She used them expertly to dissect through the intercostal muscles and pleura.

She inserted her index finger into the hole she'd made and announced, 'No adhesions. I'll introduce the cannula now, Greg. Could you pass me . . . '

He was already prepared, with the cannula held firm in the artery forceps.

'Thanks.'

Greg attached the cannula to the drainage system he'd prepared earlier and immediately, air bubbled through the water.

'No haemothorax,' he said.

'Good. It's done, Simon,' she said and she smiled as he mustered a grin.

'Are the others all right?' he whispered raggedly.

'Oh, sweetie,' she said. 'Everyone else is fine and I understand it's all thanks to you. And you're going to be fine now, too.'

The sound of rotor blades was suddenly deafening overhead. Greg looked up as the shadow of a helicopter fell across the narrow deck.

'What's this?' he said, straightening up and shielding his eyes against the sun. 'Get that thing away from here.'

'I think it belongs to a radio station,' Andrew said. 'They've probably followed the ambulance.'

As if on cue, the wail of sirens cut through the air.

'I don't care who it belongs to,' Greg growled, his eyes ablaze with fury. 'Get it away.'

'Hey,' Cara said. 'Easy.'

She stared at him and he caught her eye and glared back.

'I don't like helicopters,' he snarled.

By the time the paramedics arrived, Cara had finished suturing the wound and had anchored and dressed the cannula.

She looked up and met Greg's eyes. At least the fury had gone from him.

'Nice job. Doctor,' he said.

'Well, I think you helped a little.' She smiled, but her smile was touched with concern. Why had he reacted so vehemently to the presence of the helicopter? Surely, working in emergency medicine, he must deal with them all the time?

3

Ray raced onto the deck when it was all over and Simon had been safely removed from the ship, on his way to the nearby hospital.

'I'm so sorry,' he said. 'I've only just heard. I was . . . '

'You can explain later,' Cara said. 'Right now we need to check out these boys.'

But as she spoke, her eyes were fixed on Greg. He was watching the helicopter, which was still buzzing round the port and he looked disturbed. More than that, he looked angry.

'They're only doing their job,' she said, touching his arm. 'Just as we did. Simon's going to be fine.'

He flinched at her touch, then turned to look at her, but there was a distance in his eyes, as if he were a million miles away in his thoughts. He didn't seem to see her at all.

'Greg,' she said gently. 'Are you all right?'

'Don't they realise how dangerous it is? All these cranes . . . and what the hell do they think they're doing, flying over the port anyway? When I find out who authorised this . . . '

'Hey, Greg.' Cara laughed softly, her eyes searching his face as she suddenly found herself in the position of trying to reassure him. 'Forget them. We still have work to do here. You seem awfully hung up on safety.'

'Hung up?' he growled. 'What on earth is wrong to want a safe working environment for people? To want to prevent tragedies and save lives? I hate helicopters. Can't you see the danger they pose?'

'Frankly no, I can't,' she said.

'No, well, you wouldn't,' he said accusingly.

He glared down at Cara. His whole face had tightened with rage and he looked dangerous. But over a helicopter? Sure it was annoying, but that didn't explain Greg's fury which seemed out of all proportion.

'Because I had a run along the quayside?'

'It was a stupid thing to do.'

Ray looked from one to the other and shook his head.

'What have we got?' he asked.

'Just a few cuts and bruises,' Cara said, still distracted and rather concerned about Greg, but suddenly his mood changed.

'And a few very shocked and shaken young men,' Greg said, keeping his voice low. 'They're little more than kids and they've just witnessed something pretty harrowing. Has transport been arranged to take them home? I think that for most of these boys, a hug from Mum is all the medicine they need.'

'Yes,' Kate said. 'It's all done. And once we've cleared everyone off the deck, I'll do something about this mess.'

She looked around at the spilled luggage.

'My first thought when I saw this lot was the trouble we were going to get from the owners of the luggage,' she admitted. 'Then I saw Simon and the colour of his skin, the sweat, and I realised that at least all of this can be compensated for. You can't compensate for a life, can you? And when you made that hole in his chest — it looked so horrible and painful.'

Her lips quivered slightly.

'It's not just the boys we need to take care of, Cara,' Greg murmured. 'Kate's pretty shocked herself. Let's move everyone inside and assess them.'

He put his arm around the purser and she sagged against him. Holding her up, helping her retain some dignity, he half carried her inside and sat her down.

'I-I'm so sorry,' she stammered. 'I don't know what came over me.'

'I do,' Greg said. 'You've had a shock. But you coped, Kate. You organised the ambulance and you were calm when it mattered, so don't apologise if your legs have gone a bit wobbly on you, okay?'

She smiled up at him and nodded, his kindness bringing her to the brink of tears. Cara saw the exchange and thought how good it must feel to be on the receiving end of such kindness. Not that she'd ever know, because Cara Sanford didn't lean on anyone. Ever.

They spent the next hour checking out all those who had been on deck when the brute fell, but there were no serious injuries to deal with and the most anyone needed was a minor dressing or a cold compress.

When they'd finished, Cara looked over at Greg. His sleeves were rolled back revealing muscular tanned arms. Whatever that guy had, if he could bottle it and stick a label on it, he'd make a fortune. Well, he could if he dropped the attitude.

She walked across to him.

'I'm so glad you were here, Greg,' she told him. 'Thanks for all your help.'

'Well, this beats arguing the toss with people in a stuffy boardroom. Anyway, I was glad to be of assistance.'

'You're welcome to use my cabin if you want to freshen up,' she said. 'They don't seem to know when we'll be sailing now since there's going to be an investigation into the accident, so you've plenty of time.'

'You won't be delayed long,' Greg replied. 'The manager, Ralph Carter, won't allow too much disruption to his schedules. But I would like to use your shower, if you don't mind?'

She handed him her keycard.

'My cabin's right next to the medical centre. Help yourself to whatever you need. I'll be along shortly.'

When she finally returned to the cabin, having given him plenty of time, he was already finished. Clean and fresh and dressed again.

'You were quick,' she said.

'I thought you'd want to use the shower yourself,' he said.

'I do,' she said. 'At the rate I'm using

this shower, the ship may well face a serious water shortage.'

He laughed and picked up his jacket and briefcase.

'I'll leave you to it,' he said.

'Thanks,' she said. 'I'll freshen up then I'll buy you a coffee in the Mermaid lounge. Or something stronger if you'd prefer. It's the least I can do after all your help.'

He waited a beat, seemed to think it over, then he relaxed.

'Coffee will be great,' he said. 'I'll see you up there.'

As she stood under the shower, water crashing down around her, she told herself it was just a cup of coffee. She didn't even like the guy but he was a very good doctor and that she admired.

She had a sudden vision of her mother's face, wrought with misery and worry.

'It's just a coffee,' she said out loud. 'Since when did meeting a guy for coffee mean anything more than just having a drink, for Heaven's sake?'

She didn't have to end up like her mother. That would only happen if she opened her heart, and that was something that she had absolutely no intention of doing.

*   *   *

Greg felt peculiarly restless in the Mermaid lounge and after waiting for what seemed like an age, he returned to Cara's cabin. He thought that maybe she'd forgotten about him.

'Hi!' Cara answered his knock. She was fully dressed in olive green cropped trousers and a lime top, and she turned to gather up the bloodstained clothes she'd been wearing earlier off the floor. 'Take a seat. I'm just going to put these in to soak and do a couple of things in the medical centre then I'll be right with you. I would have to be wearing cream, wouldn't I?'

She gave a rueful laugh and left the cabin.

Greg walked round the small cabin

69

and picked up a tatty and rather ragged brown koala from Cara's pillow. One of the eyes was missing and had been replaced with a tiny button.

Something about this tugged at his heart — he couldn't explain why. It just looked so lonely sitting there on the pillow, and yet so loved, like something Cara had carried round with her since she was a little kid. And that thought touched him more deeply than he imagined possible.

She certainly didn't strike him as being either sentimental or soppy, and the toy just added yet another dimension to her.

The cabin had precious few personal items. There were a couple of paperback books, a hairbrush and an almost empty cosmetic bag on the dressing table.

There were no photographs. No reminders of home, save for the koala.

He placed the koala back and turned his thoughts to the meeting. Didn't what happened earlier prove his point?

What about the unforeseen things that happen? You can't plan for every eventuality.

And he knew better than anyone that one small thing can turn the world on its head forever. One small and seemingly insignificant thing, like having some idiot ram into the side of your vehicle when you were on the way to answer an emergency call and calling your brother, asking him to cover for you while you found another way to get to the scene — a fire at a factory where a fireman was badly hurt.

Arriving at the fire to see the air ambulance already taking off as it had done a thousand times before, rising into the billowing smoke. He'd never even considered the danger of helicopter flight until that moment when he'd looked up with a sense of dread seizing him. Something hadn't looked right — he didn't know what or why, whether it was premonition or whether something happened to make him feel that.

He just knew something bad was going to happen. And it did.

Suddenly blazing white light blinded him as something in the factory exploded and the helicopter was coming down, only bits of it visible in the swirling smoke.

He gripped the back of the chair in front of the dressing table and stared at his reflection in the mirror. In that instant of blinding white light, the helicopter pilot, Brad, the injured fireman they'd just rescued and four of George Hammond's men in the building had perished.

Nothing he could have done could have saved any of the lives lost, except one. His brother's. If he hadn't called his brother to cover for him . . . if, if, if!

It should have been him in that helicopter; his life going up in flames, not Brad's.

Cara returned at that moment.

'All done,' she said with a smile. 'Sorry it's taken so long. Hey, are you all right?'

Her smile vanished, erased by the haunted look on his face and she hurried over to him, her hand resting on his arm, the compassion in her eyes almost unbearable.

'Greg, what's wrong? Have you heard something about Simon's condition?'

He came to his senses. He hadn't relived that awful moment in such detail for a long time. He guessed it was the helicopter that had triggered it. He couldn't look at one of the damn things without remembering that night. He'd learned to cope at the hospital with seeing the air ambulance daily, watching it take off and land regularly. Somehow he managed to detach that from the image in his mind. But today, seeing the helicopter around the port, it had all come flooding back.

'Greg?'

'I'm sorry, Cara,' he said and added without thinking, 'You look wonderful.'

She looked taken aback and her cheeks flushed at the compliment. He hadn't meant to speak his thoughts aloud, but he was in utter turmoil what with helicopters and memories.

And now he'd embarrassed her.

'I'm sorry,' he said hastily. 'But you do. Much better than the crumpled, blood-stained look. I was just lost in thought, that's all. I haven't heard anything about Simon yet, but I'm sure we'll hear something soon.'

Lost in thought, and that was all? What kind of thoughts did he entertain, she wondered, that left him looking so lost and utterly devastated?

'Well, this wasn't my chosen outfit for meeting the passengers,' she said with a wry grin. 'But I seem to have messed up my Sunday best and the Captain said casual dress is okay.'

'Well, you look great,' he husked, his voice almost giving out on him.

'Shall we?' she said, indicating the door.

They were in the part of the cabin where it narrowed by the en suite and he put his hand out to her to go first.

'No you,' she said and eventually they

both moved together, then stepped sideways, laughed and stepped the other way.

'This is crazy,' he said. 'You'd think they'd give the ship's doctor a decent suite instead of putting you up in this poky rabbit hutch.'

Laughing, Cara side-stepped into the en suite, leaving the way clear for him to leave.

No sooner were they out in the corridor than a steward approached and told Cara the Captain wanted to see her.

'I'm so sorry again,' she said with a groan.

'It's okay,' Greg said. 'I'll see you in a minute.'

He watched her hurry away and wondered if he was ever going to get that cup of coffee.

4

Cara hurried to the Captain's quarters. He gave a little speech about how well she'd done and said again how glad he was to have her on board.

She felt quite on edge, aware that Greg was waiting for her and she'd already kept him waiting an age. The poor guy had got so fed up waiting in the Mermaid Lounge he'd ended up coming to find her — and now she'd abandoned him again.

She wondered at the twists and turns of fate that had seemed determined to bring them together, yet now seemed just as determined to keep them apart.

But perhaps fate had stepped in on Simon's behalf, and now its work was done.

'Anyway, I shan't keep you,' the Captain said at last and Cara was once again on her way to meet Greg.

And then she bumped into Ray.

'I'm so sorry I wasn't there when you needed me,' he said. 'One of the kitchen staff had cut himself and needed a couple of stitches. And I'd left my phone in my cabin.'

'Not your fault, Ray,' she assured him. 'You don't have to explain. Anyway, Greg and I managed fine, and you were there to help with the others.'

'Well, I just wanted to let you know that I have my phone with me now and if you need me, I can be found. Unforgivable that I wasn't able to be contacted before. I'm really sorry, Cara.'

'Don't dwell on it, Ray,' Cara said, impatient to get moving. 'Greg was there and he put together everything I needed.'

Time was ticking away. Soon the passengers would be aboard and anyone not sailing would have to leave. How embarrassing would that be if, after making Greg wait all that time, she never turned up?

But Ray still looked worried and her heart went out to him. As a health professional, he'd be feeling as if he'd let her and the patient down. He'd be dwelling on the fact that he'd been careless enough to leave his phone behind in his cabin.

He was much too nice a man for her to let him feel so bad about one minor lapse. The truth was, they weren't even officially on duty yet. Ray had done absolutely nothing wrong.

'What were you supposed to do? Leave the casualty you were dealing with? Forget it, Ray. I have. And I'm sure if Greg hadn't been on hand, someone would have found you.'

He gave her a wry smile. 'Thanks, Cara. It isn't usually as action-packed as this, I promise you. I'm all for a quiet life myself. I've done my bit in busy A&E departments and I've no wish to return to that kind of hectic life. Oh, and we've had word from the hospital,' he added. 'Simon's going to be okay. They X-rayed him immediately. You'd got the cannula positioned perfectly, but I daresay you already knew that.'

'Nice to have it confirmed though, Ray. Thanks.'

'I'll leave you to it,' he said. 'I understand Greg is waiting for you in the lounge.'

'Yes, I believe he is.'

It was good news about Simon and that made the delay worthwhile. She'd been worried about handing his care over, but the doctor who'd come to accompany him to hospital seemed more than capable of handling any further emergencies despite being on crutches herself. She was in the process of assuring her that she knew all about transporting a patient with a chest drain when Greg confirmed that fact for her.

'He'll be in safe hands with Emma,' he'd said. 'She might bash him with one of her crutches if he gives her any trouble, but apart from that he couldn't be in better hands.'

'I've a good mind to bash *you* with one of my crutches,' Emma said.

'Goodness knows you probably deserve it.'

Neither of them seemed put out or offended by her concern, for which she was grateful. And she enjoyed the friendly banter between them. It had reminded her of home and colleagues with whom she enjoyed a good working relationship.

But it would be all change when she got back. A new hospital, a new team, a new start.

She had to force herself to slow down as she ran towards the Mermaid Lounge. The last thing she wanted was to hurtle in all red in the face and breathless. But then, Greg had already seen her looking less than her best and besides, what did she care what he thought of her?

Just before entering, she spotted the young steward in the corridor and called out to him.

'Hey,' she said. 'I want a word with you.'

Was she really so formidable that she

could bring such trepidation to someone's face? Surely not? He looked
terrified.

'About before,' he said, his brow
creasing with apprehension. 'I'm sorry I
was so slow, I . . . '

'I wanted to thank you,' Cara
interrupted. She didn't want the poor
guy to grovel and he was so young, not
much older than the baggage handlers.
She wanted to put him out of his
misery as soon as possible. 'And I also
wanted to apologise.'

'Apologise?'

'I was really rather rude to you
earlier. I hadn't taken into account the
fact that you were shaken up by the
whole thing. I should have done. You
did a good job.'

'Really?' he sounded so surprised
that she gave herself a mental kick for
ever letting him think otherwise.

'Yes, really,' she said. 'And the fact
that Simon is going to be okay is down
to the team effort of everyone, including you.'

'You were really fantastic too,' he mumbled.

'Thanks.' She grinned, then turned at last to enter the Mermaid lounge.

Greg sat alone by the window in one of the blue padded seats on the sea side of the ship. He had one leg crossed over the other, his ankle resting on his knee and he leaned on one elbow, dotting his lips with his finger as if deep in thought.

He looked long and lean and even more beautiful than she remembered him. *Anyone would think you fancied him, Cara Sanford*, she teased herself, but that was nonsense of course. As she approached, he turned his eyes from the sea to look at her, then leapt to his feet, his smile warm and friendly.

It caught her unawares. She felt as wrong-footed by his smile as she had by his earlier pompous manner.

'Sorry I was so long,' she said. 'We've heard from the hospital. Simon's going to be fine.'

He held up his mobile phone. 'I

heard from the hospital too,' he said. 'And I didn't mind waiting for you, Cara.' He smiled.

He was about to say more when his phone rang.

'Do you mind if I take this?'

'Not at all.'

Why should she mind? She was at the beck and call of a mobile herself most of the time.

'Claire,' he said, turning his face away slightly. 'I'm a bit tied up right now. Is it urgent or can I call you back?'

Cara felt uncomfortable. She wondered if she should get up and move away.

'Yes, yes I will, I promise,' he said. 'Bye, yes, bye.'

He slid the phone into his pocket and smiled apologetically.

'I'm sorry about that,' he said. 'Where were we?'

Something about that call reminded Cara of life at home before her father left. The secretive phone calls, the false smiles, the endless insincere apologies.

'The fire chief thought you were a dancer,' he said when she didn't speak. 'You have the figure and the poise for it.'

He spoke so matter of factly, as if he saw her as a set of bone and muscle decently put together and well maintained. Cara felt her smile waver just a little. It was a pity he'd chosen that particular analogy for it snapped at her heart like the sting of a rubber band.

'My mother was a dancer,' she said somewhat stiffly. 'Classical ballet. Shall I get the coffee?'

'Already ordered,' he said and as if from nowhere, a steward appeared beside them with a tray.

'Sailing has been delayed by at least an hour, ma'am,' he addressed Cara as he set the cups down. 'Because of the earlier incident.'

'Thanks for letting me know,' she said and he melted away as quickly as he'd appeared.

When she turned back, it was to see Greg staring at her. He didn't avert his eyes for a moment.

'I've put my foot in it,' Greg said. 'I'm so sorry, Cara. I wish there was some way of scrubbing out the past few hours and starting again. We didn't get off to a very good start, did we?'

She took a deep breath. There was absolutely no point in telling him about her past, allowing old bitterness to sour this rather nice moment in her life. Life was full of good moments and bad ones and she'd learned over the years to treasure the good and set aside the bad.

And if he had a wife, what did it matter? They weren't doing anything wrong. Just having a coffee together. And then they'd never see each other again. All perfectly innocent. And besides, he probably wasn't interested in her anyway.

'Not at all, Greg.' She smiled warmly. 'I think you were pretty wound up about that meeting and you were right, I was being irresponsible. How did it go?'

'Meeting?' He seemed distracted,

then remembered what had happened earlier. 'I think I made my point. I didn't return for the second round, but I had my knights lined up to fight for me and I'd guess the battle was won. I was out getting some air during a break when I saw the brute break free and decided that my services might be of more use here than in a boardroom.'

'Well I'm very glad you did,' she said and reached for a cup, her hand shaking as she picked it up.

It surprised her. Her hands so rarely shook. The last time it had happened was at her mother's funeral when her estranged father put in an unexpected appearance.

Strange to compare her feelings now with those tumultuous, confusing emotions that the sight of her father at her mother's funeral had aroused. But then again, it had been a very emotional day.

'Cara, I . . . '

'Greg, you . . . '

They spoke in unison for the second time since they'd met, clattered their cups back in the saucers and laughed. She clasped her shaking hands together in her lap like some kind of prim matron.

'You first,' she said. 'Tell me about your plans for the emergency exercise. How would you like to see it done?'

'You really want to know?'

'Of course.'

And so he told her and she listened, watching his lips, his eyes, every part of his face as he spoke. She'd been right about the passion. It was there all right, running hot through his whole body, but it was for his work, nothing else.

Embarrassed, she realised he'd stopped speaking and she was still staring at him.

'I've bored you,' he said. 'I'm sorry, Cara.'

'No, no you haven't,' she said, mortified that he'd taken her silence for rudeness. 'I think you're totally right — about the unknown scenario. It makes much more sense.'

'So what about you, Cara? What are

your plans for after the cruise?' he asked.

'I'm going straight to Heathrow from the ship as soon as she docks back here,' she said. 'I'm booked on one of the coaches going to the airport. I guess this was my last day in the UK.'

'Do you have to rush back to Australia the minute you get back?' he asked casually.

'I don't *have* to,' she said hesitantly, for the first time considering her life back home. 'But I'll be moving house prior to starting my new job and of course there's a lot to do.'

'A lot of work involved in moving house,' Greg agreed. 'You'll be pretty busy and in a hurry to get back, I guess.'

'I'll need all the time I can get,' she said. 'I'm cutting it quite fine as it is.'

He seemed about to say something when his phone rang again. *Whoever she is*, Cara thought, *she has demands on his time. Big demands.*

'I'm sorry,' he said.

She watched him as he took the call, saw a veil come down over his features as if a cloud had suddenly appeared over his head. His shoulders seemed to slump a little and as he glanced at her with an apologetic smile, the light dimmed in his eyes.

'No, I haven't forgotten. It's only been a few minutes,' he said, his voice sounding so kind and patient that Cara felt as if she were melting. 'Has it?' He looked at his watch. 'That long?'

He'd been talking to Cara for ages without noticing the passage of time.

His voice was warm and reassuring as he spoke to his caller. 'Try not to worry, Claire. I'll be with you soon.'

Cara looked the other way, feeling as if she were intruding on a very private moment. She wondered who Claire was. Someone he cared about, obviously, but who perhaps was proving to be a bit of a burden if the dimming of his eyes was anything to go by.

'Yes, all right,' he said, his voice softening still further. 'I'll ring you as soon as I leave the port. And yes, thanks, of course I'll stay for supper, but I can't stay long. I have to get back to the hospital this evening. See you later.'

He pushed the phone back into his pocket.

'Sorry about that,' he said. 'Family.'

Family? Wife? Kids? What was it to her if there was? The affection had been there in his voice, though. Someone he cared a great deal about had been on the other end of that phone call. Cara couldn't even begin to explain the twinge of jealousy she'd felt. It was particularly odd, since she had always avoided close relationships in her own life. But what must it be like to have someone care about you? Not something she was ever likely to find out.

And what was it Ray had said? Something about him carrying around a lot of baggage?

None of my business, she told herself, but even as she did, she heard herself ask casually, 'Wife?'

'Never been married,' he said. 'That was my sister-in-law, Claire. I promised I'd call in and see her and my nephew Danny. She's going to give me supper, so while you're dining in style tonight at the Captain's party, think of me with my beans on toast, won't you?'

She laughed. Beans on toast sounded pretty good to her. Much more her style than formal dining.

Yet still the questions persisted. It was as if she'd totally lost control of her tongue.

'And what about your brother?' she asked, hating the false lightness in her tone, hating herself for unashamedly fishing for more information. It was none of her business and irrelevant since she was never going to see him again.

'My brother is dead,' he said and once again, he failed to meet her eyes and looked instead at his watch. 'And I really should be going.'

He got to his feet and towered over her, looking down, his eyes dark.

'It's been really interesting meeting you, Cara,' he said.

Interesting? Wasn't that what you said when you couldn't think of anything complimentary to say?

'Well, goodbye. Thanks again for all your help and good luck with getting your way over the port exercise.'

He smiled assuredly. 'Oh, I'll get my way, Cara. I usually get what I want, one way or another.'

He reached to shake her hand and somehow ended up kissing her cheek, leaving her with the scent of him, warm and earthy, to remember him by. The gesture seemed to take him as much by surprise as it did her. Then they said goodbye and he was gone, striding out of her life as quickly as he'd entered it.

So which one of them instigated that kiss? Did she push her cheek forward or did he offer his lips first?

Cara sank back into her seat and bit her lip. If only she hadn't mentioned his brother. Ah, well, too late now. Families, eh? Her mother, his brother.

Strange how those you love the most leave you with the deepest scars.

She got up again and hurried across the lounge to the port side and looked down at the dock. Passengers were moving from the departure lounge, getting ready to board via the gangway. Greg left by way of the crew's gangplank, his long legs carrying him swiftly away and finally out of sight. He didn't give the ship so much as a backward glance.

Maybe he was in such a hurry to rush to visit Claire that he'd forgotten Cara already.

She leaned her forehead against the glass and sighed.

'Oh, Greg,' she said sadly.

If she wasn't a sensible woman with her feet stuck firmly on the ground and her head nowhere near the clouds, she might have thought she'd just said goodbye to someone who could be very special. And it was horrible to think that she would never see him again.

From a purely professional point of view of course, she told herself sternly. He was a good doctor. It would have been great to have had the opportunity to work with him. That was all.

5

Greg turned his car into the drive of his sister-in-law's house at about the same moment the Princess Helena was gliding out of the dock. Cara Sanford had hardly been out of his thoughts since he left the ship. Cool, distant and certainly not interested in him. He'd almost bored her to tears talking about his pet project.

But what else did he have to talk about?

The front door opened and before he'd even switched off the engine, his two-year-old nephew was running out to greet him.

As always, along with a surge of love for the little boy, Greg also felt the weight of guilt settle around his shoulders. It should have been his brother driving into the drive to be greeted by this child. And it hurt more than anything to know that Danny had never known Brad, and that the closest thing he had to a father was Greg. And an uncle was a pretty poor substitute.

He got out of the car, stretched out his arms and gathered Danny up, swinging him high in the air. Since the accident, Claire had been over-protective and living in a state of constant anxiety. She'd lost her husband and was terrified of losing her son.

Before the accident, Claire had been a consultant in geriatric medicine. Not the most glamorous job, but she'd been dedicated to her profession and had achieved extraordinary rates of recovery, particularly among her stroke patients.

Now she couldn't even leave the house to buy a loaf of bread unless someone went with her, and she'd never shown any interest in returning to work.

She'd been heavily pregnant with

Danny when Greg broke the news of Brad's death to her. At first she'd been unbearably calm but eventually calm had turned into something else. Something destructive. And it was eating away at her still.

Greg set Danny back down, then reached into the back of the car for the flowers he'd picked up on the way there.

'Give those to Mummy,' he said, handing them to Danny. 'Tell her she loves you.'

Danny rushed off and presented the bunch of flowers.

'You love me,' he said.

'Oh, I do,' Claire said. 'I love you more than anything in the whole world.'

She took the flowers and buried her nose in them.

'They're lovely, Greg. What's the occasion?'

'Just thought you sounded as if you needed cheering up a bit,' he said.

'I think Danny misses you,' Claire remarked as they all went inside. 'He only ever seems to come alive when you're here.'

She was pale as always, with dark hollows under her eyes as if she hadn't slept.

'Have you tried going out today, Claire?'

She looked away and hurried into the kitchen where she began to fuss with the flowers.

'Claire?'

'I — I haven't had time,' she said.

It was an excuse. One he'd heard a thousand times before. Claire had spent the whole of the summer at home.

'He needs to get out, Claire,' he said gently. 'And so do you. He needs the stimulation of other kids, different places and faces. And in a few months he'll be joining a nursery.'

'Don't say that,' she cried, slamming her hand down on the draining board. It was as if he'd said Danny was to be taken away from her. Then she turned back and regarded him with anxious, hollow eyes.

'You will stay for a while, Greg? You said you'd have supper.'

'Just for an hour,' he said. 'Then I have to put in some time at the hospital.'

Greg lifted Danny up and buried his nose in his tummy making him scream with laughter. It was the most wonderful sound in the world, one his brother would never hear — and it was all thanks to him.

★   ★   ★

The lifeboat drill hadn't exactly been hitch-free. One of the elderly male passengers had fainted in the heat and had grazed his legs in his fall. Cara and Ray had attended to him at once and he was none the worse for his ordeal. In fact, he was the first to insist that such drills were a necessity for the safety of all on board.

Afterwards, when the ship set sail, Cara stood on the deck among the passengers watching the land retreat into the distance. She was still staring into the distance when the Captain came to stand beside her.

'How are you?' he asked. 'Everything all right? You have all you need on board?'

'Yes, thank you,' she said.

'I'm sorry our meeting earlier was so brief,' he went on. 'You did a great job. And you had assistance from Greg Harding. I would have liked to have thanked him too, but with the delayed sailing I was rather tied up.'

Cara took a deep breath. 'Well, I hope something is going to be done about port safety,' she said. 'An accident like that should never have happened.'

'You're quite right and the last I heard, Greg was kicking up hell about it.'

'He was?'

'Oh, yes.' The Captain laughed. 'And believe me, Greg Harding in full flow is a force to be reckoned with. Which brings me rather neatly to another matter. I'm afraid we're likely to encounter some pretty rough weather fairly soon,' he went on. 'That could mean that you're kept quite busy for the first few hours with cases of seasickness. We're sailing into a storm and it appears to be gathering strength. But we should pass through it quite quickly and from then on, it will be plain sailing.'

'I'm glad to hear it,' Cara said emphatically.

He smiled briefly, nodded, then departed and Cara realised that if she was going to be in for a busy time, she should get herself down to the medical centre.

She hadn't been to her cabin since before they left port, and decided to stop by to brush her hair and freshen up after standing up on deck. As soon as she opened the door, the scent of flowers hit her. On the dressing table stood an arrangement of summer flowers in a basket.

'Oh, how lovely,' she exclaimed.

'Who would send these?'

Some kind soul. Perhaps Simon's parents as a thank you for saving their son's life.

There was no card with the flowers. Well, they almost certainly weren't from him — from Greg — and why would they be?

She couldn't remember the last time a guy had sent her flowers. How very kind of someone, she thought. Perhaps the shipping company had sent them. Perhaps all female crew found flower arrangements in their cabins. She touched one of the soft blooms and smiled. They were lovely.

* * *

'I wasn't expecting it to be as rough as this,' Cara said ruefully after seeing yet another passenger complaining of feeling seasick a few hours later. 'I'm not feeling too hot myself.'

She had sat down to dinner earlier, but had been unable to eat anything as her stomach lurched and quivered along with the ship.

She'd even resorted to taking one of her own remedies, but it had made little difference. If she didn't start feeling better soon, she'd have to have an injection. They worked extremely well, but she wasn't keen on needles!

'I must admit, it's pretty bad,' Ray agreed. 'The Captain will have changed course slightly. I don't understand the science of it, but apparently it's best to be facing a certain direction in strong winds so the waves don't hit broadside. Or that's my understanding of it. She's a pretty stable little ship. It shouldn't get any worse than this.'

'I hope you're right, Ray. I don't mind telling you, my earlier reservations have turned into full-blown regrets.'

Ray laughed. 'Tell me that tomorrow when you're stretched out on the sun deck or when you're first in the pool for an early morning dip.'

'What makes you think I'll be taking a dip?'

'Cara, it's obvious you like to keep fit. There's not a lot of space for running on board and I don't see you working up a sweat in the gym. You'd be bored out of your skull within two minutes. It's my guess you'll be doing several lengths of that pool every morning. Am I right?'

'Once again, yes,' she said. 'Am I really so transparent?'

'You Australians are famed for being water babies,' Ray said. 'I've yet to meet one who isn't into surfing or diving.'

They were interrupted by someone ringing the bell of the medical centre, but Cara was grateful to Ray for momentarily taking her mind off the heaving ship.

Ray opened the door and a couple in their sixties entered, the man keeping a protective arm around his wife. The ship lurched and they both staggered sideways. The woman was pale and clutching her arm. Ray took up position on the other side of her and they helped her to a chair as Cara came out from behind her desk.

'It's my wife's arm, Doctor,' the man said. 'She was feeling a bit under the weather in our cabin, so we thought we'd go to the lounge bar. We were on our way there when she lost her balance and fell. I'm sure I heard something crack.'

'It's a lot of fuss,' the woman said sharply, made irritable by pain and fear. 'I just want to go back to my cabin. No, forget that, I want to go back home. I want to feel solid ground under my feet again. I wish we'd never booked this cruise.'

'Let's have a look, shall we?' Cara said, gently taking the woman's wrist. 'Could you give Ray some details, Mr . . . ?'

'White,' the man replied. 'I'm Philip White, and this is my wife, Patricia.'

'I don't want to be any trouble,' Patricia said, looking close to tears as the ship juddered alarmingly.

'It's no trouble, Patricia,' Cara answered gently. 'It's what we're here for.'

'It's not broken, is it?'

'I'm afraid it probably is,' Cara said. 'We'll do an X-ray to confirm it, but I believe you have a Colles fracture of your wrist.'

'Oh, trust me,' she said wearily. 'Our first holiday for thirty years and I have to go and do something like this.'

She smiled weakly as her husband returned to her side and reached across and squeezed her other hand reassuringly.

'So this is your first cruise?' Cara asked. 'Mine too. Ray assures me that this time tomorrow we'll all be sunbathing on deck. I'm really looking forward to that.'

Patricia mustered a smile. 'Not half as much as I am,' she said. 'Even if I do end up with one white arm.'

The X-ray confirmed the fracture and Cara told Patricia this as she sat on one of the beds.

'Will I need an operation?'

'Just a small one.' Cara smiled. 'The fracture requires manipulation and I'm afraid you'll then be in plaster for up to six weeks. The good news is — ' the ship lurched alarmingly and Cara paused for a moment. 'The good news is that I can do all that for you right now, and you can carry on and enjoy the rest of your cruise. How long since you ate or drank anything?'

'Hours,' Patricia said. 'I was so nervous before we boarded the ship I couldn't eat or drink. It must be, what . . . ?'

'About eight hours at least,' Philip said.

'Good.'

The ship lurched and Patricia let out a squeak of alarm.

'Don't worry, darling,' her husband soothed. 'This is nothing compared to how it was in the Navy. Sometimes it'd feel as if the ship wasn't touching the water at all. We'd seem to fly across the waves and then land with an almighty bump.'

'And that's supposed to be reassuring?' Patricia gulped.

Cara left her patient sitting on the bed and went to confer with Ray.

'Given Patricia's medical history, she's not a suitable candidate for a Biers Block.'

'Haematoma block, then?' Ray asked. 'I thought so. I'll prepare a tray.'

'Let's hope no one else needs us for a while,' Cara said.

'That's why there should be two nurses,' Ray muttered. 'I should have touched wood.'

'So you're to blame for all this.' Cara laughed. 'You and your tempting of fate.'

Suddenly the ship tipped backwards, seemed to hang suspended then crashed down with a judder and a thud.

'What was that?' Cara asked Ray, trying to stay calm.

'A big wave probably,' Ray said, unconcerned. 'You get used to it. But it won't last long. We'll soon be through it and floating on water like a mill pond.'

He looked across at Patricia and gave her a wink when he said that and she gave him a rather anxious little smile in return.

'I hope you're right, Ray,' Cara murmured. 'I don't think my stomach can stand much more of this.'

Cara could understand Patricia's anxiety. She was feeling more than a little nervous herself. Not least at having to perform an operation, however minor, when the floor kept disappearing from under her feet. It was like trying to work on one of those theme park rides with the sliding floors.

'If it's any consolation, this part of the ship is the most stable,' Ray said. 'Stuck in the middle here, we get the least roll. That's why the medical centre is situated where it is.'

'Somehow Ray, that doesn't reassure me,' Cara returned. Because if it was this bad at the most stable part of the ship, what on earth must it be like elsewhere?

★   ★   ★

'Time you weren't here, Greg.'

He looked up from his desk and saw Emma Scott hobbling towards him. She was late, but he wasn't going to pull her up about her timekeeping, especially since she'd covered for him earlier when he was at the port meeting. But it would take more than a plaster-encased foot to keep Emma from coming to work.

'How's the foot?'

'Itching like crazy and driving me mad.' She laughed. 'I think you trapped a few ants in there when you put me in plaster. Probably did it on purpose to torture me. But I'll cope. You'd best get off home now, Greg. It's pretty wild out there. How's it been here?'

'Normal sort of evening,' he said, closing the file and tossing it onto the pile on his desk. 'It's quietened down in the last half hour or so.'

'I doubt it'll stay that way,' Emma warned. 'There's a big old tree down in my village, which shows how bad it is. I daresay there'll be some weather-related injuries overnight.'

'Cheerful soul.' Greg grinned.

'How about you? How did the meeting go?'

'I managed to miss half of it,' he said. 'But I finally got my point across. We're going for a completely unscripted exercise this year. I've put the date up on the board. Apart from the date and the time, we won't know what we're dealing with.'

Emma threw back her head and laughed. 'Just as well that jumped-up port manager didn't know what he was dealing with when you first walked into his boardroom a few years ago.'

'What's that supposed to mean?' Greg feigned offence.

'You know very well. You may have been off-form for the past couple of years, but I bet today the poor guy didn't know what had hit him.'

Off form? Had he? Yes, he supposed he had. And Emma, with whom he had worked closely for a number of years, probably knew that better than anyone.

He got up to leave.

'So how come you got involved with Simon on the ship when you were supposed to be in the boardroom? I didn't get a chance to ask earlier. Didn't have anything to do with Cara Sanford, did it?'

'I have no idea what you're talking about,' he said, but the chilly act didn't work on Emma. She'd known him too long.

'Pull the other one — it's got bells on. When we were getting Simon into the ambulance, you two were sparking off each other like a couple of hot electrodes.'

Greg shook his head and changed the subject back to work. Emma couldn't be more wrong. All he seemed to do was irritate the life out of Cara.

'It's been pretty quiet here for the past hour. But you'll call if you get swamped?' he said. 'Don't try to cope alone.'

'Aww, worried about me, Greg?' she teased.

'Not in the least,' he said with a grin.

'But I promised your husband I wouldn't let you overdo it.'

'Well as of now, you're on leave, remember? I don't want to see you back here for a fortnight.'

'You should be so lucky,' he returned. 'Call me if you need me. Promise, Emma?'

'Clear off,' she said. 'Go on, before I call security and have you thrown out of the hospital.'

He left with Emma softly chuckling behind him.

It was only as he left the hospital that he realised just how bad the weather was. He hoped it wasn't like this out at sea, or Cara would be having a bad time of it. Not that the weather mattered too much on board ships these days. And a small one like the Princess Helena was just as capable of weathering storms as one of the bigger vessels. Better, probably, being not so high-sided.

He switched the radio on and frowned. She'd have her flowers by now. Almost as soon as he got in the car after leaving the florist, he had regrets. He didn't even know why he'd sent them, except she seemed lonely somehow and that bleak, poky little cabin looked as if it could use some colour.

And there was that tatty little koala. The sight of it had haunted him.

The voice of the late night DJ on the local radio station gave a weather update. The storm had caught everyone unawares with its violence. A nearby road bridge had been closed and the port had been forced to shut down operations, cancelling all sailings. Several trees were down and there had already been some structural damage to property.

Perhaps the Princess Helena hadn't sailed after all. It was quite possible, after all the delays, that she was still in port when the order came to shut down. She could well be anchored out in the harbour ready to sail the next day.

6

'Something's wrong, Ray,' Cara said after the lights dimmed briefly. It wasn't just the lights. Something was different, something had changed and she couldn't put her finger on what it was. 'Can you feel it?'

'Engines have stopped,' he said, looking up at the ceiling as if it would provide an answer. 'I can't be sure, but I don't think that's a good sign.'

That was it! The constant low thrum beneath her feet had ceased. You became used to it very quickly, but noticed when it had gone.

Cara smiled at the nurse. She was getting used to him already. He had a tendency towards being a bit of a prophet of doom and she found it curiously endearing. He had a rather sad face too, pulled down somehow by his beard, which made him look more doom-laden than ever.

But she had the feeling that under that stiff, rather formal exterior beat a heat of gold. She'd already seen that warm heart in action — not just with the patients, but with herself as well.

'I'm going to have one last check on Patricia, then I'll let her go back to her cabin,' Cara declared. 'She'll be much more comfortable there.'

The ship was still rolling, but now there seemed to be no rhythm to it. What a way to wind up her round-the-world adventure, adrift in a storm off the south coast of England. *Way to go, Sanford*, she thought, *why didn't you just take the ferry across to the Isle of Wight for your maritime adventure?*

There were two beds in the medical centre and Patricia was on one of them, her husband sitting beside her on a chair.

'How's it feeling?'

'I can't feel anything really,' Patricia answered.

Cara checked Patricia's fingers.

'No discomfort?'

'None.'

Just as she let go of Patricia's hand there was a massive jolt, then a lurch which almost threw Cara right off her feet.

'What on earth was that? Did we hit something, Ray?'

'Wave,' Ray said. 'Hitting us. Another big one.'

Even Philip White, who up until now had seemed unconcerned, looked alarmed.

'We've lost the engines, haven't we?' he said.

'Seems so,' Cara said. 'But not to worry, eh?'

Despite her brave smile, Cara had seen the apprehension on Philip White's face. He was an ex-Royal Navy man. He'd know perhaps better than anyone the real danger they were in.

The ship had barely recovered before yet another wave slammed into them, making the whole vessel shudder again.

'I was going to suggest you return to

your cabin,' Cara told Patricia. 'But I think you would be safer staying here until the storm passes. I don't want to risk you having another fall. You're welcome to stay with her, Philip, but I'm afraid I can't offer you the other bed in case we need it later.'

She asked Ray to give him a blanket and a pillow so he could at least make himself comfortable in the chair, then she returned to her desk. She was more frightened than she cared to admit, even to herself. The sheer violence of the storm had taken her completely by surprise.

'Why don't you go to your cabin and try and get some sleep, Cara?' Ray said. 'I'll hold the fort here and I can wake you if you're needed.'

'No, it's all right, I . . . '

'It's pointless both of us being up. I can catch up on my sleep in the morning. Usually after a night like this, everyone stays tucked in their cabins until lunchtime.'

She sighed. She was tired, it was true.

It had been a strange and busy day, one way and another.

'If Patricia decides to go back to her cabin . . . '

'Yes, I know,' he said. 'I'll give her the talk about warning signs to look out for. And I'll tell her to exercise her fingers as much as she can. Get some rest, Cara. You look all in and we're likely to be busy later if this continues. You should grab some sleep while you have the chance.'

She said goodnight to the Whites, then went along to her cabin. It was just as well the Whites had decided to stay put, she thought, as she was tossed from one side of the corridor to the other. Just putting one foot before the other was difficult. One minute the floor dipped sharply ahead of her, the next the ship tilted to the side and just as quickly she'd be fighting against falling backwards.

Her cabin was right beside the medical centre, yet it was taking her an age to get there.

'Doctor — are you all right?'

She looked up to see the Captain heading towards her. He seemed to be making a better job of walking than she was and guessed that was what was meant by having your sea legs.

'I was going to try and get some sleep,' she explained, stopping outside her cabin.

'I doubt you'll get much rest,' he said. 'I've just come to warn you. We've got an engine failure. They're trying to fix it now, but while we're without engines, we can't comfortably ride the storm. To be honest, we're as helpless as a piece of driftwood.'

The ship rose, fell with a crash then lurched to the side. It seemed to be almost a pattern.

'Is there a possibility of the ship capsizing?' Cara voiced her worst fears.

'No, no,' he said. 'The worst that will happen is that we're all extremely uncomfortable for a few hours. You may get some calls to visit passengers in their cabins and if you do, please contact the bridge and we'll send someone to escort you. We expect to have the engines back soon, but until then it's going to be pretty unpleasant.'

She nodded, her mouth dry. Her stomach was feeling decidedly queasy.

'We'll wait until morning to break it to the passengers that we're returning to port,' he added. 'We've sustained some damage, broken glass mainly, and it's going to be best for all concerned if we get back home as quickly as possible.'

'What about the cruise?'

'These things happen,' he said. 'Thank God, not very often. The passengers will be offered a refund or an alternative cruise. I'm afraid it'll be the end of your cruising experience, though. Not exactly a great memory to take back to Australia with you.'

'Ah, well.' Cara responded with a shrug. To be honest, she couldn't wait to get off this heaving ship.

And as she let herself into her cabin, she couldn't believe that she had such an utterly selfish thought as to actually feel pleased at the prospect of returning to port.

She opened her cabin door and was practically thrown inside.

The sight that greeted her was a shock. The flowers were scattered around the cabin as if someone had plucked every one from the reservoir block and just thrown it into the air.

She found the basket, placed it upright and tried to poke the flowers back in, but it was difficult to do anything with the movement of the ship and her stomach feeling as if it was about to heave. She felt sick right up behind her eyes, if such a thing was possible. She'd never felt like this in her life. From now on, she vowed, she'd be a lot more sympathetic towards patients complaining of motion sickness.

She didn't bother to undress, but just lay back on the bed and closed her eyes, clutching her little koala to her chest. The spinning in her head was worse. It would be better to be on deck in the fresh air when feeling like this, but Ray had told her while they plastered Patricia's arm that when the weather was this bad, the outer doors were bolted so that no one could venture onto the decks.

As the ship rolled heavily, Cara slid up her bunk, banging her head on the wall at the end. The next moment she was sliding towards the other end. She'd noticed straps on the bunk when she'd first boarded the ship and had laughed to herself. She'd wondered why on earth anyone would need to strap themselves into bed. Now she knew. But she wished she didn't.

There was no way she was going to sleep in this. With a sigh, she got up and finished clearing up the flowers, then went into her en-suite. It was even worse in the close confines of the small shower room. She didn't have to move at all to bump into the sink or the toilet. How on earth must the older passengers be coping? she wondered. Some were in wheelchairs, others barely mobile at all.

Back in her bunk she braced herself in an effort to stop her body from moving up and down. Was this the point where she was supposed to start assessing her life? The point when life flashed before your eyes like a series of movie stills?

She saw hers in stark black and white. It began with a picture of her parents, her mother tall, willowy and beautiful and her father, also tall, handsome and rather distant. But was the distance something she now added with the benefit of hindsight? Now that she knew the truth about him?

Another picture formed in her mind of her mother looking wistfully at an old photograph album with tears running down her cheeks. As well as pictures, there were newspaper clippings. Yvonne Sanford had been hailed as the most promising young dancer of her generation. But Cara's father had insisted she give up her career for love, for marriage, for their only child, and she had done so willingly.

Other snapshots raced through her mind. Her father, the powerful, popular surgeon, kissing the cheek of a pretty young woman at a party. Her mother's tears afterwards. His long absences, her mother's long depressions, the bitter arguments when he was at home and finally, his packing up and leaving while his latest girlfriend, not much older than Cara, sat outside in his car waiting.

Cara had watched her mother fade over the years, but once the marriage was over, she crumbled completely. Shattered into tiny pieces, her battered heart no longer able to sustain life. Her will to live gone, along with her dreams.

Cara bit her lip, realising she was close to tears. But it was her life. It all happened during her formative years. She started out at university a very bitter and wary young woman who buried herself in her studies, and later her work, in order to avoid having any kind of romantic life.

There were no great romances to look back on. A lot of close friendships, a lot of lives saved, but her heart remained safely under lock and key. No man would ever break her, the way her father had broken her mother. No man would ever get that close. She would never give up the career she had worked so hard for, for anyone.

No chance of love jumping in to ruin her life. These days most men back home assumed she was either married or in a steady relationship, and she was happy to let them think that.

Common sense told her that no man was worth giving everything to. If a man she adored as much as she'd adored her father, her own flesh and blood, could let her down, then what chance of love with any man?

'This is ridiculous,' she said and not wishing to be alone with her thoughts a moment longer, returned to the medical centre only to find Ray on his way out.

'I was just coming to get you,' he

said. 'One of the engineers has been hurt. They're sending a couple of seamen to come and escort you down there. Would you like me to stay here or come with you?'

'What's the nature of the injury?'

'He's had a blow to the head, I believe.'

'Then I think you should come with me,' she said. 'We'll take a spine board, surgical collar and head blocks. Can you find someone to man the medical centre while we're away? Someone with some first aid skills, if possible.'

'I'll get on to it,' Ray said. 'And as well as that, we've had several requests to visit people in their cabins. Nothing urgent, but a number of minor injuries.'

'Okay. Well, the head injury gets priority right now.'

Barely three minutes later, two young seamen arrived at the medical centre.

The whole thing had a surreal feel to it. She felt almost drunk, as if she was watching all this unfold from the outside and it was happening to someone who looked like her, spoke like her, but wasn't her at all.

One of the seamen offered his arm.

'Thanks,' she said. 'But I think I'll be better moving along under my own steam.'

'Baptism of fire for you, isn't it, Doc?' He laughed. 'This isn't the best thing to happen to a cruise virgin.'

Cara smiled, despite him using that hated word. *Virgin*. It conjured up someone young and shy, or someone old and dried up! And she was neither of those things, just a person who had chosen not to have a sex life. She'd been close — she wasn't completely without feeling, but had always man-aged to escape relationships before things went that far. Her mother told her that once a man possessed you in that way, there was no escape — not if you loved him. And it wasn't the kind of trap Cara was going to fall into.

In all the years she'd avoided intimate relationships, some of her friends had been through two or even three marriages. She bit her lip. It felt like a hollow sort of boast. *Look at me, everyone, I don't know if it's better to have loved and lost because I've never loved. How about that then?*

'Well, it would have been nice if you could have arranged better weather,' she said brightly, forcing the smile she knew would quickly become genuine. 'Or at least tried to keep the engines going.'

Both seamen laughed. Cara joined in, although the last thing she felt like doing was laughing. There was nothing like being tossed about like a ping-pong ball in a washing machine for bringing all your hang-ups, regrets and deepest fears charging to the fore.

'Could you tell me what happened in the engine room?' she asked them.

'It's the Chief Engineer,' the man walking beside her explained. 'He lost his balance and was thrown backwards. He's hit his head and it's bleeding, but he seems to have hurt his neck and back as well.'

'I see,' Cara said. 'Did he lose consciousness?'

'He may have done, but not for long.'

They reached the reception area and headed for the stairs.

'We don't use the elevators in these conditions,' the seaman explained.

'Sounds good to me,' Cara murmured.

They seemed to descend forever, going further and further down into the bowels of the ship. The air felt different and the storm had less effect down there. The smells of paint and engine oil and a dozen other things that Cara didn't recognise filled her delicate nostrils.

The engineer was lying on the floor, his teeth clenched with agony. Around them men worked, trying to restore the engines.

'It's my back,' he croaked raggedly. 'Hurts like hell, Doc.'

'I'll give you something for the pain,' Cara told him. 'And we're going to get you on a spine board. It's important we immobilise you as soon as possible, especially the way this ship is rolling. Did you lose consciousness at all?'

'I think I blacked out,' he answered.

'Okay,' she said. 'My name's Cara. I think we met earlier when I did my tour of the ship. You're Clive, aren't you?'

'Yes,' he confirmed.

She carried out her examination quickly, then turned to Ray.

'He has a depressed skull fracture,' she said. 'But that's not my immediate concern. I'm more worried about spinal injury. This is probably going to sound like a stupid question, Ray, but is there any chance of getting him back to shore?'

'We may be able to get air sea rescue out here,' Ray said. 'But transferring him to a helicopter in this wind with a possible spinal injury? Tricky to say the least.'

'I don't think we have a choice,' Cara said as she got to her feet. 'Right, I need three strong guys to help me and Ray get Clive safely onto this spine board. Any volunteers?'

7

Greg picked up the phone on the second ring and reached for his jeans when he recognised Emma's voice.

'I'm so sorry, Greg,' she said. 'I really hate having to call you out, but you're the only person for this job.'

'I'll be there as soon as I can,' he said, cradling the telephone between ear and shoulder as he pulled on his jeans. 'What is it?'

'That's why I'm sorry, Greg,' she said and he just knew she'd be biting her lip right now. 'It's not here, it's a call-out.'

He paused, straightened up and took the phone from under his ear, squeezing his fingers hard around it.

'Air ambulance?' he said, his stomach knotting.

'Grounded because of the weather,' she said and he wondered if she could feel his relief filtering along the phone line. It didn't matter anyway, because what she said next rekindled his tension. 'It wouldn't be any use in this instance anyway. I'm sorry, Greg, but it's the air sea rescue helicopter and they need a second doctor on board. The police are clearing it for landing on that school playing field near your house — they're sending an officer to pick you up. Is that okay?'

His mouth was dry, so dry he could hardly speak. He moistened his lips.

'Sure,' he said and then another thought occurred to him, an even more worrying one if that were possible. 'You said air sea rescue. Does that mean it's out at sea?'

'Stricken cruise ship,' she said. 'Without engines, at the mercy of the storm and a crewman with a skull fracture and possible spinal injury. There is one casualty on board with a fractured wrist, but she doesn't require evacuation. I'm sure more minor injuries are likely and it may be that you'll have to be left on board once the

133

casualty has been evacuated. I'm really sorry, Greg. If there was anyone else I could call out, I would. But you're both capable and available.'

'Which ship?' he asked.

'The Princess Helena,' Emma replied. He realised he'd almost expected her to say that and had braced himself for the jolt. 'And it sounds like they're having a pretty bad time of it from what I can gather.'

He'd seen Cara at work, knew her judgement was spot-on and her skill second to none, but that didn't stop that knot of fear tightening in his stomach — and it was fear for her as a fellow doctor this time, not for himself. A ship with numerous casualties aboard was bad enough, but a drifting ship in a ferocious storm was something else.

He hung up and finished getting dressed just as there was a knock on the door. He opened it to a blast of wind and a policeman holding out a set of overalls and a harness.

'They said you were to put these on

here,' the policeman explained. 'They said you'd worn them before and would know how to fit the harness.'

Yes, he did. He'd done it dozens of times before — but not once in the two years since his brother was killed. But this was not the time to dwell on the past. His mind was firmly on the future and on the patient stuck on that stricken ship.

He would have responded to this emergency call anyway, but knowing Cara was there, possibly in danger, almost certainly working under dreadful conditions, pushed all other fears to the back of his mind.

He was ready quickly.

'Let's go,' he said. 'I don't want to waste any time.'

★ ★ ★

It was like a scene from a disaster movie, but all too real. Cara looked around the wreckage of the lounge bar. Glass littered the floor and the efforts to clear up were being hampered by the sea coming in through the shattered windows. It was mainly safety glass from the windows, but Cara saw a few shards from broken glasses and bottles scattered about.

How on earth are we going to get this guy off this ship? she thought. But she knew that the helicopter crew would be experienced and capable.

She saw Kate directing the clean-up with an almost ice-cold calm. She seemed to be coping very well with this.

It was the noise Cara found the most difficult to cope with. She could stagger against the sudden, harsh movements of the ship, but the noise was almost deafening.

The pounding of the waves, the roar of the wind, the creaking of the ship and the occasional smash when another window gave way to the power of the sea were just the more obvious of the noises — there were other sounds she didn't recognise.

It was only now, as she saw the

devastation at first hand, that she realised the extent of the predicament they were in. And it terrified her.

It was an awful admission to make, even to herself, but she was scared. Not just for herself, but for everyone on board this ship. She knelt down and spoke to the man secured firmly to the backboard. Getting him up here from the engine rooms had been quite a tricky operation, but they'd managed to transport him with minimal discomfort.

'All right, Clive?' she said bracingly. 'The cavalry are on their way. I hope you don't mind heights. We've got you all ready to be evacuated by helicopter.'

'I must be bad if you're taking me off in this weather,' he replied, looking grim.

'Simply a precaution, Clive,' she said calmly. 'Anyway, I don't want you cluttering up my medical centre in your oily overalls.'

He laughed, but Cara noticed his teeth chattering. He was scared, too. And he had every right to be. He was about to be dangled above the sea in this raging storm. It seemed like madness, but he couldn't stay here.

She felt Ray's hand rest on her shoulder as he bent down to whisper in her ear. He'd been visiting the passengers who had requested medical assistance.

'I'm sorry, Cara,' he said. 'I've dealt with most of them, but there are a few you should see, including another suspected broken wrist.'

She got to her feet slowly. 'Okay,' she said, smiling at the steward who was acting as an escort. 'How long until the helicopter gets here?'

'Fifteen minutes. But you don't need to be here, Cara. There's an RAF medical officer on board and a civilian doctor, both trained in emergency procedures. I can handle things this end if you want to check out the others.'

'You're a star, Ray,' she said and he handed her a bag.

'Just call me Sirius,' he said without cracking his face. 'The brightest star in the sky.'

She grinned. 'I won't argue with that.'

'I've made a list of who you have to see and the advised order, and I've packed up everything I think you'll need. Try not to worry, Cara. The crew are extremely experienced and capable. I know how bad it seems, but we will come through this.'

'Thanks.' She nodded. 'That's good to hear.'

'Well, it's true.'

Cara knelt down beside Clive again.

'Ray is going to stay with you now, Clive,' she told him. 'I have to check out some other passengers. I may not see you again before you leave, but I just wanted to say goodbye.'

'Thanks,' he said. 'Good luck to you, Cara. You're going to need it. But it's true what Ray said. It will be okay.'

★ ★ ★

'Good to have you aboard, Greg.' Jim Cardy, the MO, slapped Greg across the shoulders as he strode through the blue light-slashed darkness towards the waiting Sea King. Sparks of white, red and blue light bounced off the driving rain. 'What do you know?'

'The Helena is in trouble and an injured crewman needs airlifting off,' Greg said, his heart in his throat as he bent double to run beneath the whooshing helicopter blades. 'Is there more I should know?' he added at a shout.

'There is more,' Jim said once they were aboard.

'The wrist fracture?'

'That and mounting minor casualties. They're going to need you on board, Greg. The ship's doctor is going to be overwhelmed. She'll need all the help she can get. They only have one nurse aboard as well, which is making things even more difficult than they should be.'

Greg smiled, despite the tension. He couldn't imagine Cara ever being overwhelmed by anything. But he could see that his presence might be useful at the very least.

He felt no fear as the helicopter rose into the wind. But since seeing his brother killed in the helicopter crash, he'd steered clear. Death didn't frighten him, but dying and leaving Claire and Danny even more alone than they already were terrified him.

If anything happened to him, who would take care of them? Claire's was not a close-knit family and he had the awful feeling that if anything happened to him, and Claire went completely to pieces, then Danny would end up in care.

He'd never analysed this before and it seemed a strange time to be doing it now. But that was the stark and brutal truth. He wasn't free, not even to die. As long as Claire and Danny needed him, he'd be there for them — and nothing, not even a beautiful doctor with Wedgwood-blue eyes, was going to change that.

Then why send flowers? Because it

seemed like a nice thing to do, that's all. Unfortunately that was all it could ever be.

Jim shook his shoulder and gave him a thumbs-up sign. They were almost there.

The clouds parted momentarily. The moon lit up the sea and there she was, the Princess Helena, being tossed about on mountainous moon-silvered waves like a child's plastic boat in a bath.

The vessel looked so small down there. So vulnerable and so very alone.

*   *   *

'Such a lot of trouble to go to over a finger,' the merry old gentleman said as Cara finished buddy-strapping his fingers. 'You must be so busy out there.'

'No problem,' she assured him. 'And it may be broken. I'll be able to tell more when I can X-ray your hand. In the meantime, I'd like you to wear a sling which will keep your hand elevated and reduce any swelling.'

'Such a silly thing to do,' he went on. 'I fell against the wall, that's all.'

'You'll have to make up a better story than that to tell your friends back home, Harry!' Cara laughed as she quickly fitted him with a high sling. 'And I don't want you to attempt going to the medical centre until this ship is stable, okay? If you need me before then, just call and I'll come to you.'

Harry was the last patient she had to see. She had no idea of the time, but was pleased to have reached the end of Ray's list. As she'd carried out her visits, the steward assigned as her escort waited patiently outside each cabin.

'That comfortable, Harry?'

'Very,' he said. 'How about you?'

'Me?' She was surprised by the question. She was aware that she looked a bit dishevelled and somewhere along the line she'd managed to rip the pocket from her shirt, but this was the first time anyone had asked how she felt.

In between visits, she'd been thrown down corridors and had fallen twice. From the amount of times she'd smacked into the guard rails that ran along the corridors, she felt sure she must be black and blue from head to toe. Once she'd tripped up the stairs, striking her shins. The resulting swearing had made the steward escorting her giggle. Her head was pounding and she wasn't sure if it was as a result of hitting it on a door, or caused by the relentless movement of the ship.

'Yes, you,' Harry persisted. 'You look beat, if you don't mind me saying, and that's a nasty bruise on your forehead.'

'Bruise?' She touched the tender area with her fingers. 'It's nothing. I bruise really easily.'

'And you keep holding your middle,' he added.

'Do I?' Well yes, she was aware of a bit of tenderness there too, but it was hardly surprising. She rose to leave and suddenly the cabin swirled and she had to sit straight back down again.

'Whoo,' she said. 'That was a bad one.'

Harry shook his head, looking concerned. 'I think you need a doctor yourself,' he said. 'The ship barely moved then. The storm seems to be abating.'

Cara laughed off the idea. She'd never needed a doctor in her life. Why should she need one now?

'Nonsense,' she said. 'I'm perfectly fine. You can take more painkillers in four hours if you need them, okay?'

She stood up. It had been an exhausting night and it was far from over. She couldn't afford to let a few aches and pains slow her down.

The steward wasn't outside the cabin, but was further along the corridor standing at one of the bolted doors looking out. She joined him.

'The helicopter is here,' he said. 'You can just about see from here.'

Cara pressed her cheek against the glass and looked out and up to see a man being winched down. It was horrible to watch. He looked so helpless hanging there.

'I should get out there,' she said. 'They may need some help with the casualty.'

'Sorry,' the steward said and pulled a scrap of paper from his pocket. 'We have another call to make.' He peered at her. 'Are you okay?'

'I'm fine,' she said quickly, keen to get moving. 'Are you?'

'Me? Of course I am,' he said.

'Well then,' she returned. 'All fine. That's good, isn't it?'

The next call didn't take long. The passenger was having a panic attack. Her husband had also panicked, thinking his wife was having a heart attack. The pair of them were in need of reassurance which Cara was pleased to give, nothing more.

'Where to now?' the steward asked.

'Back to the medical centre, I guess,' she said. 'Is it me, or are things getting better?'

'The wind seems to be easing,' he

said, frowning at her. Cara was beginning to think she'd grown two heads. 'But it's probably temporary. Are you sure you feel okay, Doc?'

'You know,' she said, irritated at the way he kept peering at her, 'I could make my own way back from here. You may as well try to grab some rest. You've been great, thanks for your help.'

She hurried away from him. There was still quite a lot of roll, but the violence seemed to have gone out of it. She took an inventory of her own aches and pains as she headed back. Sore ankle. Maybe she had hurt it more than she thought yesterday — was it really only yesterday, a few hours ago, that she'd fallen over like an idiot in front of Greg Harding? That windy day filled with sunshine seemed like a lifetime ago.

Griping knee. More than that. It protested with every step she took. Various bruises all over her body. And sore ribs. Oh, and the head, mustn't forget the head, she thought. The giddiness was because she was tired, and nothing more sinister than that. And although she was used to being tired, used to working until she was operating on autopilot, she'd never before felt this crushing, all-consuming weariness.

She had to pass the reception area which led off to the lounge bar. In the distance she could see Ray, looking small and slight as he spoke to a guy in overalls. The guy wore a helmet and a harness and there was something about him — the way he stood that made Cara's heart somersault.

Oh Lord, Cara thought. *What is this? Some kind of hormonal crisis? Am I going to start swooning over every masculine-looking guy I see?* The professional in her wanted to go down the corridor, check everything had gone okay with the evacuation and say hi to the helicopter guy. The woman in her wanted to turn and run, and she probably would have done too if the ship hadn't lurched at that moment and sent her spinning on her way.

How could I think anyone looked sexy in that get-up? Those overall things are hardly flattering and I couldn't even see his face. It could have been a well-built woman underneath all that for all I knew. I must be tired, she decided. Tired and halfway to madness.

★   ★   ★

The medical centre was empty. Mrs White had gone. Ray had been back here and had written on Mrs White's notes that he'd sent her back to her cabin. And there was no updated list of patients to see. But Cara had no intention of going to bed. The night wasn't over yet, and it would be easier to keep going for a few more hours than give in.

She slipped into her cabin, tried to tidy herself up and realised it was a lost cause. She then made her way back up to the lounge bar where the clean-up operation was still going on, but there was only Kate working now. Ray had vanished and the guy from the helicopter had gone. Probably on his way back to shore at this very moment.

She looked around. The damage was greater than it had been last time she'd been up here.

'Did Ray say where he was going?' she asked.

'Oh, hi, Cara.' Kate straightened up and rubbed her back. 'He said he had one or two calls to make.'

Suddenly the ship lurched, flinging Cara forward and slamming her against the bar. She was still getting her breath back when she heard a pitiful scream.

She looked around and saw Kate sprawled on the floor, already trying to pick herself up.

'What timing,' Cara said as she made her way towards the purser, glass crunching under her feet. 'I'm really glad you waited for me to get here before doing that.'

Kate looked up at Cara, her face streaked with blood, then looked down at her right arm and began to shake violently.

'What have I done?' she wailed.

'You've cut yourself, Kate,' Cara said. 'Your arm looks worse than it is, but it'll need stitches. Stop looking at it, Kate. Look at me instead. There, I'm better to look at than that, aren't I?'

Kate nodded.

'I know you'd prefer some hunky guy to look at, but you'll have to make do with me I'm afraid,' Cara went on, keeping her tone light as she checked out the laceration in Kate's arm. It was deep, really deep. She then examined Kate's face, but the wounds there were superficial, except for one on her forehead which was the one producing all the blood. It would need three or four stitches.

'I'll do a very neat job, I promise you. But I'd prefer to do it in the medical centre. I want to irrigate your wounds properly.'

The steward had been right and the lull in the storm had been temporary.

Now it seemed to have mustered up all its strength to begin another onslaught.

Awful juddering seemed to have replaced the constant rolling. It felt almost as if the ship were in her death throes, as if she were shuddering violently before falling apart completely.

Kate wouldn't stop staring at her wrist. She was holding her arm out and shaking.

'Kate,' Cara said sharply. 'Look at me.'

Kate snapped her head up. Tears were making streaks through the blood on her face.

'Good girl. Can you walk?'

Kate's lip wobbled and she nodded. This on top of the shock she'd had earlier had just about tipped her over the edge. The poor woman was quietly distraught.

'Okay, I want you to lean on me. And if at any time you feel you want to stop, you tell me.'

It wasn't far from the lounge bar to the medical centre, just down the one set of stairs. Kate leaned heavily on

Cara all the way, her arm squeezing round Cara's aching ribs. Cara held Kate's arm up for her and together they managed to keep on their feet.

Ray, please be in the medical centre this time, Cara thought as a wave of nausea swept over her, seeming to pass from her scalp all the way to her feet. Things still felt unreal, but now there was a different element. A feeling of not quite being in control of things.

She reached for the door and saw a figure standing over by her desk.

'Ray,' she said. 'Thank goodness you're here.'

The figure stepped forward and it was only then that she realised he was much too tall to be Ray, far too wide in the shoulders. He was wearing jeans and a black T-shirt and he looked even more gorgeous than he had yesterday. And then she saw the discarded overalls on the floor.

'Ray's not here,' Greg said. And for the second time he asked her, 'Will I do?'

8

She couldn't believe this was happening again, that once more he appeared just as she needed him. She really had never been so pleased to see someone before in her life.

'But what are you doing here? How did you get here?'

'I flew,' he said as he moved forward and helped lead Kate towards one of the beds. She sat and he lifted her feet onto the bed, then he turned and began to gather all they'd need together, setting things out on a tray, keeping his hands and his eyes busy as if he didn't want to look at her. Cara watched him, relief engulfing her, and at the same time she felt an acute sense of loss.

How could you miss something you'd never had? It was all so confusing, and she was finding it difficult enough to think straight without Greg Harding here to mix her up even more.

'I thought you didn't like helicopters?' she asked.

'I don't,' he replied. 'But they thought you might welcome an extra doctor on board, so here I am. At your service.'

The implication was that she couldn't cope on her own. Yet she'd managed the worst of it and she was still standing — just. She tried to stop herself, but she had already started to bristle.

'Well you've had a wasted journey,' she said coolly. 'And you don't have to do that. I can get Ray.'

'Ray's seeing some patients,' he said and she realised he was just as cool. 'You'll have to make do with me.'

Kate looked from one to the other, confused. Hurt as she was, she could sense the atmosphere between the two doctors.

Cara smiled at her, anxious to reassure Kate that the sudden twanging tension in the air was nothing to do with her. They weren't hiding anything from her, nor were they unduly concerned about her injuries.

'You comfortable there, Kate?' she asked brightly, rather too brightly perhaps.

'As comfortable as can be expected,' Kate replied. 'Isn't that what you doctors say?'

Cara squeezed Kate's uninjured hand. 'Something like that,' she said. 'Any questions you'd like to ask?'

'Will it hurt?'

'Not if I can help it,' Cara said as she washed her hands. 'I'll use a local anaesthetic before I suture the wound.'

'How about permanent damage?'

'You'll have a scar,' Cara answered. 'But that's all you'll have as a reminder of this. And I'll make sure it's as unnoticeable as possible.'

Greg, who had already washed up and donned gloves, began to prepare a syringe. What Cara had thought of as intuitive teamwork now began to sniff of interference. Who did he think he was, coming in here and virtually taking over her territory? He didn't even have to feel around, but seemed to know exactly where to lay his hands on everything he wanted.

Cara had to regain control. This was her patient, her call. Greg's assistance would be handy, but she didn't need him. She didn't need anyone.

She opened her mouth to speak but he beat her to it. 'I've added epinephrine.'

Which was exactly what she was going to tell him to do. He'd thought ahead of her. But it would be silly and childish to get annoyed about it.

'What does that mean?' Kate asked.

'Lidocaine is the local anaesthetic we'll use,' Cara explained. 'The epinephrine will decrease the blood flow and it'll help prolong the effect of the anaesthetic.'

Cara had every intention of injecting the local anaesthetic herself, but Greg was already doing it.

She wanted to feel annoyed, but

couldn't find it in herself as she watched him at work. It was as if there were two Caras battling under the surface. The Cara who had fought all her life and who wanted to carry on fighting, and the weary, hurt woman who wanted to hand over responsibility to someone else and curl up in a corner somewhere and just go to sleep.

If it had been anyone else but him, the weary woman might have won.

He took care not to pierce the skin, injecting the Lidocaine under the skin edge and using the same stab point to inject in several different directions.

So he liked to minimise the discomfort of his patients as much as possible, she thought. He wasn't one of these gung-ho types, enthusiastically stabbing the skin in an attempt to get the anaesthetic into the patient as quickly as possible.

'There,' he said when he'd finished. 'Now to wait five minutes, then we can get on.'

He turned his attention to Kate's head.

'A lot of superficial cuts,' he remarked more to himself than anyone else. 'That big one looks worse than it is. That can be closed with strips.'

'Oh, can it?' Cara said stiffly, the fiercely independent doctor in her fighting to be back in charge. If Kate had been an unfeeling object and not a person, Cara might have insisted on stitching the forehead just to be bloody-minded. But Greg was right. Closure strips would be perfectly adequate.

'You disagree?' he asked, still managing not to look at her. She was having no such problems. She'd hardly taken her eyes off him since the moment she saw him and it annoyed her intensely that he wouldn't look up and meet her angry glare.

But she didn't really know why she was angry. She'd never felt this way before in her life.

'No,' she said and for the first time in her entire working life, she felt as if she were floundering. How dare he make her feel so small?

She had to regain control of the situation. 'I'm going to use interrupted sutures on Kate's arm,' she said to Greg. 'If you've no objection?'

'Go ahead,' he responded. 'It's your call.'

Yes, she thought. *It is. Please remember that.* And after the thought had passed through her mind, she wondered if she'd spoken aloud, for Kate was staring at her and giving her a strange look.

'Would you like me to irrigate?' he asked.

'Yes, please,' she said.

'Okay,' he answered and somehow managed to make that one word of acquiescence sound like a condemnation.

Then he turned to Kate and smiled, explaining to her that the wound would have to be thoroughly cleansed before going any further. She'd stopped looking so scared and shaken, Cara noticed. She seemed more interested in what was going on between Cara and Greg.

He turned away to fill a syringe with sterile saline and Kate leaned towards Cara.

'What's going on between you two?' she whispered:

'Nothing,' Cara answered.

'I might have a hole in my head and a gash in my arm, but I'm not daft. You're acting as if you don't like each other, yet only yesterday you seemed to be getting along so well. I mean, ghastly as it was, the way you two worked together yesterday — well, it was like watching a ballet with every movement perfectly choreographed.'

'I've no idea what you mean,' Cara murmured under her breath. 'I don't even like the guy.'

'How can two people who have only just met behave as if they have a past?' Kate demanded. 'Are you sure you two met for the first time yesterday?'

'Absolutely,' Cara said.

Greg returned then and got on with

cleansing the wound. Several times he asked Cara to pass him forceps so he could take out tiny pieces of glass. His hand was steady and almost unaffected by the constant movement. He seemed to time every action to coincide with the brief seconds of near stillness.

'It's a clean cut,' he said to Cara. 'You won't need to excise the edges.'

'I know,' Cara said tightly.

'Good.'

She pressed her lips together, wishing she knew what she'd done to deserve this sudden cooling off, little knowing that he was thinking much the same thing.

He hadn't expected her to run into his arms when she saw him, but had been quite taken aback by her aloofness and her apparent displeasure at seeing him, not to mention the state she was in.

He wished he hadn't sent her the damn flowers. He wasn't given to making those kind of gestures as a rule, never had been, but he'd wanted to do something. A goodbye gift, that was all. Perhaps that's why she was being like this. Maybe she didn't like flowers. Or maybe she didn't like *him*. That was the more likely explanation. She hadn't mentioned them and, call him old-fashioned, but it was customary to thank someone for a gift.

He almost laughed out loud. *Just listen to yourself, Harding. You didn't send the flowers hoping for thanks and besides, Cara Sanford has probably got other more pressing things on her mind right now.*

'I'm going to put in some absorbable sutures first, Kate,' Cara explained. 'The wound is quite deep and I want to close the deeper layers before I close the skin. It'll make for a neater scar in the end.'

She set to work, burying the knots as she drew the tissue together. She blinked and shook her head as Kate's arm blurred in front of her. She blinked again, squeezing her eyes shut.

'Are you all right?' Greg asked. He

wasn't looking at her so must have sensed rather than seen her hesitation.

'Fine,' she said, gritting her teeth.

'It can't be easy with the ship bucking and heaving,' he said. 'If you want to take a break . . . '

'I don't need a break,' she said shortly. 'Could I have more light here, please?'

He angled the light towards her and she thanked him.

She tasted salt on her lips as she continued. Sweat? And was that a tremor in her hand just now? She blinked and sweat stung her eyes. It wasn't hot in here, was it?

She felt the cool touch of a damp cloth against her forehead.

'Better?' Greg asked.

'Thanks,' she said. 'I won't be much longer, Kate.'

'I can't feel a thing,' Kate said. 'Take as long as you need.'

Cara battled on for another five minutes and it really did seem like a battle. Her mouth was dry, her head swimming and her body felt as if it had just about all it could stand of the relentless movement of the ship. She really should hand over to Greg. Common sense told her that. But sense, common or otherwise, seemed to have deserted her.

'I'm just going to get a glass of water,' she said. 'Please, excuse me for a moment.'

She turned from the bed. Her head felt like mush. She'd been tired before, goodness knows everyone got used to being tired working in emergency medicine, but this felt like something else.

The ship rolled and she went with it, going forward just as the floor rose to meet her. Desperately trying to stay on her feet, she leaned back and the ship lurched again, propelling her forward. Her foot caught on something and she went flying, landing awkwardly against the sink and ending up in an undignified heap on the floor.

She knew what she'd done immediately, having treated enough of these injuries in her time. The pain was quite intense and she ground her teeth together until it subsided a little.

'Are you okay?' Greg was with her in an instant. 'Stupid question. You're obviously not.'

For the first time he looked at her properly and she saw those green eyes flinch. Now what? Why did people keep looking at her like that?

'Cara,' he exclaimed. 'You look bloody awful.'

'You don't look so terrific yourself,' she muttered under her breath, referring to the dark shadow of stubble on his face.

'What was that?'

'Nothing,' she murmured.

'How did you get that bruise on your forehead, Cara?'

'Can't remember,' she slurred.

He tried to lift her arm so he could help her to her feet and she yelped.

She swallowed back a ball of pain. It seemed that now she'd acknowledged the pain, all the other injuries clamoured to be noticed too.

'Is she all right?' Kate called anxiously from the bed. 'Do you need any help?'

'Stay where you are, Kate,' Greg instructed. 'I can manage here. Cara, I'm going to get you over to the other bed and . . . '

'Finish Kate,' Cara said impatiently. 'Don't leave her sitting there half done. She's the patient, not me.'

'I will finish Kate,' he said. 'But not until you're comfortable and I have no intention of leaving you sitting on the floor however much you might want to sit there feeling sorry for yourself.'

'Sorry for myself?' she gasped.

'From the look of you, you have every right to feel that way,' Greg said, his tone softening and losing the condemnation. 'Why didn't you tell me you were hurt?'

'I'm not hurt,' she protested. 'At least I wasn't until I fell onto the damn sink!'

He put his arm round her waist and she flinched and bit hard on her lip to stifle a cry of pain.

'Ribs? Did you do that just now?'

She shook her head. 'Ages ago. I may have a few bruises.'

'A few cracked ribs, more like,' Greg muttered.

She tested her foot on the floor and winced.

'Ankle?'

'And knee,' she said ruefully. 'I'm a bit of a mess.'

'You can say that again,' he said and before she had a chance to say another word, he'd swept her up into his arms and was carrying her across to the second bed.

* * *

Cara had done a neat job of Kate's arm so far and Greg finished it off, then applied skin-closure strips to the wound on her head. While he worked, Cara lay on the next bed in silence, staring up at the ceiling. He knew her well enough already to know it was unlike her not to be trying to direct operations, or at least keeping an eye on him to make sure he did the job to her standard.

He glanced across at her and felt a surge of sympathy. No wonder she'd been so offish with him. She was in pain. And he in his conceit had thought it was about him and his stupid bunch of flowers.

She turned to look at him and her eyebrows rose as if she'd forgotten he was there.

'Greg,' she whispered. 'Did you use interrupted sutures?'

'Of course,' he said.

'What does that mean?' Kate asked.

'Don't look so worried, Kate,' he said. 'We use interrupted sutures so that if the wound later becomes infected, it's an easy matter to remove one or two stitches. We're not expecting your wound to become infected, it's simply a precaution.'

'Is Cara all right?' Kate persisted.

Cara had closed her eyes and was biting her lip.

'I'm fine,' Cara answered, without

opening her eyes. 'As I keep telling everyone, there's nothing wrong with me.'

Greg looked at Kate and lifted his eyebrows. Any fool could see she wasn't fine at all. Goodness knows how long she'd been struggling through, ignoring the pain. If he'd known she was nursing so many injuries, he would have taken charge and insisted she leave Kate's treatment to him.

He was just finishing off when Ray came in.

'What's been going on here?' he asked when he saw Cara. 'You look as if you've been run over by a bus.'

'Thanks,' Cara said dryly.

'As for you,' he turned to Kate, 'I only had to follow the trail of blood to find you.'

'I left it specially,' Kate quipped.

'Ray, would you take Kate back to her cabin, please,' Greg said. 'I haven't given her any aftercare advice, so I'd be grateful if you'd handle that.'

'Sure,' Ray said, holding out his arm

to Kate and helping her off the bed. He looked at her arm, then at her face. 'Neat job. Oh, and we've got engine power back. We should be home in a few hours. It's still going to be a rough ride, but it won't be half as bad as it has been. The men have been amazing. And women,' he added with a wink at Kate. 'The whole crew's pulled together. I've a few more people to see, but I won't be turning in. There's no point.'

Greg saw Ray to the door and when he turned, Cara was back on her feet swaying slightly and very unsteady as she leaned on the bed with both hands in order to take the first few steps.

'What do you think you're doing?'

'You heard him.' She opened her bag and began to restock with essentials. 'There are more people to see. I can't leave him to manage on his own. He's been working all night.'

The arrogance of the woman was unbelievable if she thought that they couldn't possibly manage without her when she could barely walk without grimacing with agony. She coughed and clutched her ribs.

'Are you crazy? You're in no state to take care of yourself, let alone patients. And I'm here to help out if Ray needs it.'

Cara glared at him and carried on chucking things in her bag with her left hand. Her collar bone was broken, her right arm useless. What use did she think she could possibly be?

'I think I can decide how capable I am,' Cara retorted as she picked up a stapler from her desk and waved it at him before dropping it into her bag.

Greg walked across to her and grabbed her hand to stop her throwing in anything else. He reached into her bag and took out the stapler.

'So what are you going to do? Staple people better?'

She stared at the object as if she'd never seen it before. Her forehead creased and for a moment, she looked completely and utterly lost.

'Cara,' he said gently.

She continued to stare at the stapler, then she turned her eyes to him.

'I . . . ' she began, then licked her lips quickly as she looked again at the stapler, almost as if she hoped it would have changed into something else, something she could explain.

The bewilderment in her eyes was painful to see.

'You're hurt, Cara,' he said, cupping her face in his hand. 'You've done a great job tonight, but now it's your turn to be looked after, okay?'

She dragged her eyes up to his, swallowed hard, then nodded. Once more he carried her back onto the bed, careful not to touch the areas that were painful, which seemed to be just about everywhere.

'When you hit your forehead, did you lose consciousness?' he asked.

'Can't remember.'

He shone his penlight first in one eye, then the other.

'Pupils equal and reactive to light,' he said.

'Of course they are.'

'From now on, you stay on this bed and you do not move off it, do you understand?' he said firmly. 'If you won't obey orders, you'll only prolong your symptoms and do even more damage to yourself than you have already.'

'Yes, Doctor.'

He had the feeling she was mocking him.

'Oh, one more thing,' he said. 'What's your full name and your address?'

'Cara Yvonne Sanford,' she said. 'And why do you want my address? I'm going to be moving in a couple of weeks anyway.'

He grinned. 'Good enough for me,' he said. 'Now let's start patching you up.'

9

Cara sat trembling and hurting while he cut off her shirt and tossed it on the floor.

'We'll start with your collar bone,' he said, his fingers moving expertly across the long slender bone. 'Definitely broken.'

'You don't say.'

'Are you going to comment on everything I say?'

'Probably.'

'And will you approve if I tell you I'm going to strap you up in a figure of eight?'

'As long as you do it firmly enough.'

'I may have to put a bandage over your mouth,' he threatened. 'If only to keep you quiet.'

Cara didn't want to smile. She didn't feel like smiling, but her smile had always been her first line of defence and now she was unable to stop herself. He smiled back at her, then he winked. He seemed far more relaxed than he had yesterday. Was this the real Greg Harding?

'How bad a break is it?'

'It's as you would expect,' he said. 'Broken in the mid section of the bone. They'll do full X-rays at the hospital when we get back, but I doubt there'll be any complications. There's no obvious damage to nerves or blood vessels in the area. You have good muscle tone, you're fit. It should heal pretty quickly without recourse to surgical intervention.'

'Good,' she murmured. He was back to seeing her as bone and muscle again. Component parts. No more than that.

'Are you ready? You're happy with me doing this?'

'Of course.' She nodded. She swallowed, her throat dry.

Cara closed her eyes and tried to distance herself from the touch of his fingers, the brush of his hands, the warmth of his breath as he strapped her shoulders into position. She tried even harder to distance herself from her own thoughts.

At one point, he leaned her against him, his chest supporting hers. She welcomed the support of the bandages and the support of his body, but she felt woozy. Whether it was her injuries or the pain relief Greg had administered earlier, she wasn't quite sure. She'd looked at him in horror when he'd prepared a needle.

'You don't like needles?' He'd realised at once. 'Look the other way, love. I promise you won't feel a thing.'

Doctors should never make promises like that, but after a few seconds he told Cara it was done and he'd been right.

'Is that comfortable?' he asked when he'd finished strapping her arm.

'Very,' she conceded. 'Thank you.'

'There's some heavy bruising around your ribcage,' he remarked. 'Ever broken your ribs before, Cara?'

'No,' she snapped. 'And I haven't

broken them now. They're just badly bruised.'

'If you say so,' he said, grinning.

She wished he wouldn't do that. When he grinned like that, he looked like a human being. He went to a cupboard and took out a neatly folded cotton gown which he slipped over her shoulders. He'd taken care of her dignity earlier, and for that she was grateful.

He moved his attention to her knee, bending it gently, testing the joint.

'There doesn't appear to be any swelling or damage,' he said. 'But I'll put a support on it.'

He went in search of a tubular bandage and an applicator and once again he was touching her, his hands soft but firm as he applied the support.

The relief was almost instant. Finally he checked her ankle.

'It's very swollen,' he said. 'And it isn't the one you twisted yesterday, is it? You believe in spreading your injuries around, don't you?'

'I did it on purpose,' she said.

Despite the pain, she was aware of his hands supporting her foot, his fingers gently probing. It was almost like a massage, warm and pleasant and extremely soothing. She'd heard it said of some doctors that they had healing hands, and it certainly felt as if Greg was one of them.

'All of these bandages,' she murmured sleepily. 'I will look like a mummy.'

'Feels better though, doesn't it?' he asked.

She nodded.

'Get some rest, Cara. Try to sleep. We'll be home before you know it.'

'Home? Where's home? What's going to happen to me now?' she wondered aloud.

'What was that?' Greg asked, leaning forward.

What was that smell? It was nice. Familiar. Ever so faint.

But this was no time to be thinking about scents. Far more important things to worry about. What was going to happen to her for a start? It was a question she'd often asked herself as a child.

Coming out of those school gates, searching for her mother's face among all those others and more often than not, not seeing her there.

The first few times it happened, her stomach had knotted with fear as she'd searched among the waiting parents before running for home in a panic. The first time her father found out, and he threatened to take Cara away. But away where?

After that, Cara made sure he didn't find out again.

After school, she'd run home, make her mother a cup of tea, then tackle the washing-up. At first she used to have to stand on a kitchen chair to do it while her mother sat, still in her dressing gown, at the kitchen table, staring into space. She'd shove laundry from the tub into the washing machine, then tug at her mother's arm.

'Which buttons do I press, Mummy?'

Eventually, at some point, her mother would emerge from her trance and start moving about.

'Oh, my goodness, where did the day go?' she'd say, as if losing a whole day was a normal occurrence. 'Cara, how did you get home? Did you walk on your own?'

And Cara would lie. 'No, I walked with Sarah Daniels.'

'Oh, good. You mustn't walk home on your own, darling. Silly Mummy. I won't forget tomorrow. Everything will be all right.'

And Cara, trusting little soul that she was, would believe her.

Anger rose inside her. She'd hated her mother sometimes and her father had allowed her to hate her, when all the time it was his fault. He was the one who'd made her like that. He was the one who'd destroyed the woman that she was.

'Don't stay with her, Cara,' he'd advised on the day he walked out.

'You'll never make anything of your life with her holding you back.'

But her mother had never held her back. Not wittingly, anyway. In fact, it was probably thanks to her mother and her illness that Cara was so independent.

'Where else would I go?' she'd asked her father.

'Well, your grandparents . . . '

Not with him. He didn't want her. Yet he didn't want her mother to have her either.

'Leave me alone,' she said.

But he was touching her arm, shaking her.

'Come on, Cara . . . '

She tried to push him away, but it hurt to move. She wasn't a kid any more, but a young woman and this was her mother's funeral. He'd been insensitive enough to bring his new wife along with him to pay his respects. Respect? The man didn't know the meaning of the word. And if he had been in possession of the merest shred of decency, he would have kept away.

'I told you, leave me alone,' she rasped. 'Don't you even touch me. I hate you.'

'Cara?'

It wasn't her father's voice. And she wasn't at her mother's funeral. She opened her eyes. Pain seemed to close in from all angles. She welcomed it. The physical pain was preferable to the agony of her memories.

For a second, she was confused by her surroundings, then a familiar face swam into view and it all came flooding back.

'Greg?'

'We'll be docking shortly,' he said, thankfully making no mention of what she'd said. But perhaps she'd just thought it. Perhaps she hadn't said it out loud at all. 'There's a cup of tea for you here. When you're properly awake, we'll talk about what happens next. Would you like help sitting up?'

She tried without him, but couldn't do it. And she hated feeling so utterly helpless. Helpless was the one thing she had never been.

'There's nothing wrong with accepting a little help, Cara,' Greg reasoned, and he lifted her so effortlessly into a sitting position that she was almost there before she realised it. He even managed to plump up her pillows before leaning her back.

'Can you hold the cup?'

She stared at him.

'Of course I can hold the cup,' she huffed.

But the cup weighed a ton. Without a word, he helped her support the weight.

'Small sips, Cara.'

'I've got a broken clavicle,' she snapped. 'I haven't lost my marbles completely.'

To her consternation, he laughed. He'd had a shave. And a shower. Some time during the journey back to shore, he'd found time to freshen up. His hair was still damp and he looked wonderful. How was that possible?

'Hey, there's nothing funny about this. I'm supposed to be starting a new job in just over a fortnight and look at me.'

'I am looking at you,' he said. 'And I certainly don't think you should fly back to Australia in two weeks. You're going to need time to recover from this.'

He sounded so sure of himself, so certain.

Well, if he thought he could be stubborn, he'd met his match. Nothing was going to come between her and this job she'd worked so hard for — nothing! Not cracked ribs, broken collar bones or Greg Harding. No way!

'I am going back to Australia as per my schedule,' she said.

'Okay. Well in the meantime, I'm going to admit you to hospital and we'll get some X-rays done. They'll want to keep you in for a day or two. After that, we'll see what happens.'

★ ★ ★

Before they disembarked, Ray came to say goodbye.

'Brief but memorable,' he said. 'I won't ever forget this trip.'

'Me neither,' rejoined Cara with considerable feeling.

'The steward you had with you told me you took several tumbles, but it hardly slowed you down. No wonder you collapsed, Cara.'

'I didn't collapse,' Cara protested, casting an accusing glance in Greg's direction. 'The sink attacked me.'

'I don't envy them at the County Hospital,' he remarked. 'You're going to be a right pain in the neck as a patient.'

'You can bet on it.' Cara grinned.

'Well, take care,' Ray said, stooping to kiss her cheek. 'I've written my address on a card and left it with your things. Keep in touch. See you around, Greg.'

Greg said goodbye and saw Ray to the door.

She felt sad as she watched Ray leave. The adventure was over just about a day after it had begun. She'd left port with such high expectations and she was coming back on a trolley.

'He means it,' Greg said, coming over to give her one last look before they left the ship. 'Once Ray's made a friend of you, he stays your friend for life.'

'You sound as if you know him.'

'Ray and I go back years. He's a damn good nurse.'

It took Cara a few moments to realise he was smiling. She smiled back.

There was a knock on the door and two paramedics entered.

'She's all yours,' Greg said. 'She has mild concussion, cracked ribs, broken clavicle, sprained ankle and mild ligament injury to the knee.'

Cara wasn't really listening.

'This is ridiculous,' she grumbled. 'Wasting these guys' time on me. I can walk.'

She was still protesting as they carried her off the ship and loaded her into one of the waiting ambulances.

*   *   *

'It was you, wasn't it?' Claire said soberly. 'I knew it was you. I heard it on the radio and I tried to ring you and when you didn't answer, I just knew.'

'I couldn't let you know, Claire,' he said. 'It was the middle of the night and look, I'm back and I'm fine.'

As soon as he'd realised he hadn't got his mobile phone with him and that there was no way for Claire to contact him, Greg had made his way to her house. He'd hoped she wouldn't have heard about the rescue and if she had, that she wouldn't have put two and two together, but she was still sharp, still perfectly capable of working things out for herself.

'You promised me you wouldn't go out in the helicopter,' she said. 'What would happen to Danny if you got yourself killed?'

'Don't you mean what would happen to you, Claire?' he asked, drawing away. 'Isn't that what you're really scared of?'

'Me, Danny, what difference does it make? Do you think I like living like this? I feel so trapped, Greg. And I know what it's doing to Danny, but I just can't change. I just feel so frightened.'

Greg put his arm around her shoulders, wishing he didn't have to keep doing this. If only he could persuade her to see a counsellor, but she refused all help, relying only and totally on him. He could see himself still being here, still trying to keep her head above water, in ten years' time. He didn't want to pass the burden on to Danny, and would move heaven and earth to make sure that didn't happen.

He wanted Danny to grow up as normally as possible. He wanted him to have a life, a proper life, and he was going to stick around to make sure he did.

'Where is Danny?'

'In the garden,' she said. 'Playing in the sandpit.'

'On his own?'

She let go of his shirt and pulled back from him. He hadn't meant her to hear the censure in his voice.

'I'm not stupid, Greg,' she said softly.

'I've been out there with him until you arrived.'

As if on cue, Danny came in from the garden. His face lit up when he saw Greg and Greg's heart lifted at the sight of him.

'Uncle Greg!' he yelled and ran at him, smacking into him like a soft missile and wrapping his skinny arms round Greg's legs. He was smothered in sand from the sandpit and he believed in sharing.

Greg ruffled his fair hair, so much like Brad's, and gulped back the lump in his throat. How he loved this kid — and Brad would have done, too. He'd have been a terrific father.

He looked at Claire. She'd changed so much since Brad's death. He'd like to see her leading a normal life again, too. He'd like to see her working back at the hospital. She was missed, and her skills were needed more now than ever.

'Come back to work, Claire,' he said softly. 'Just do a few hours every week.

The hospital needs you.'

'I can't,' she whispered.

'You can,' he urged.

'You just want me off your conscience,' she said bitterly.

Greg turned away from her, swept Danny up under his arm and carried him out into the garden before he said something he might regret.

It wasn't true that he wanted them off his conscience. He just wanted to see Danny out and about, mixing with other kids, not caged in this back garden like a pet rabbit. If Claire wouldn't do it for herself, then she had to do it for Danny, but every time he tried to make her see that, she used his guilt as a weapon against him.

Danny was shrieking with laughter as Greg deposited him in the sandpit.

He looked back at the house where Claire stood, as white as a ghost, and as frail as one of the elderly patients she used to care for.

'Come on, Claire,' he called. 'Come and join us.'

She stepped outside and walked over to him.

'I'm sorry, Greg,' she murmured. 'I shouldn't have said that. It wasn't fair.'

'You're a good doctor, Claire,' he told her. 'A really good doctor. What isn't fair is that all your dedication and talent is going to waste. Life goes on, and we have to move on with it. You can't spend the rest of your life grieving.'

For a moment, he glimpsed the old spark in her eyes.

'Neither can you, Greg,' she said sadly. 'But what else can we do?'

He wished he had an answer.

He spent a few minutes playing with Danny while Claire watched from the garden bench, then he got to his feet and brushed the sand from his jeans.

'You're not leaving?'

'I have to get some sleep,' he said. 'I've been up all night and I'm going into the hospital in a few hours.'

'No you're not,' Claire said. 'I spoke to Emma earlier and she said you're officially on two weeks' leave. She doesn't want to see you within a mile of the hospital. I'll make dinner, then you can get a good night's sleep and in the morning I'll make you breakfast. It's the least I can do for you. I don't know how else I can ever repay you for what you've done for us.'

'All right.' He smiled softly, too tired to argue, but it grieved him when she talked like that, talked of owing him, of debts. The debt was his to pay. 'Thanks, Claire.'

While Claire cooked, Greg took Danny upstairs for his bath and got him into his pyjamas. Ten minutes after putting Danny into his cot, the toddler was fast asleep, his dark lashes curling against his rosy cheeks, his lips curled into a smile. He let out a little sigh of contentment. His eyelids were slightly pink, a sign that he was tired.

Greg was tired, too. He leaned over, kissed his nephew's forehead and whispered, 'Night, night, little guy. God bless.'

Then he pulled up the bar of the cot

and quietly left the room.

'Great timing,' Claire said as he joined her in the kitchen.

'What's this?' Greg said, looking at the spread before him. He frowned. All these fresh salad vegetables. He didn't remember buying any of this. And was that a fresh bakery loaf on the board? 'Claire?'

She smiled at him. 'I walked to the farm shop today,' she said. 'I took Danny in his buggy. It wasn't far, I know, but . . . '

Greg went to her and hugged her.

'It's a start, love,' he said. 'A great start.'

'Well, we all have to start somewhere. Brad wouldn't want us putting our lives on hold. And you're right about Danny, he does need to get out and about. Wasn't I always telling my elderly patients that they needed to get out as much as possible? Even if it was only to stand outside their own front doors?'

He looked at her, the way she stood

with her chin jutting, and wondered how many times she had tried to make that trip to the farm shop, how many times she had got as far as the front door and changed her mind. But it didn't matter. What mattered was that she'd done it, and if she didn't leave the house for another week, another month, she'd taken that first important step.

'Now,' she said. 'Sit down and eat. That bread is wonderful. And you can tell me all about Cara Sanford.'

He sat down. 'Cara? What about her?'

She reached for a slice of bread and began to butter it.

'Emma seemed to think she was something special,' she said casually.

'Wait until I see her ... ' Greg muttered.

'Well, is she?' Claire asked.

'Is she what?'

'Something special?'

He smiled awkwardly. 'You and Emma are such a pair of gossips,' he grumbled. 'But I must admit, Cara would fit in well. She's just as bloody-minded as the rest of you.'

'I'm glad to hear it.' Claire smiled. 'So when do I get to meet her, then?'

10

'We met before,' Cara observed. 'You were the doctor who came in the ambulance for Simon.'

'Well!' Emma laughed. 'I was just about to ask you some memory test questions, but I hardly think I need to.'

Cara looked around her. She wasn't sure how long she'd been in the hospital. She knew she'd spent quite a lot of time sleeping, but the sun was streaming in through the window and there was no sign of the storm. It seemed quite late in the day to Cara, and she felt surprisingly refreshed and eager to get out of bed.

'I feel so much better,' she sighed, stretching out her legs gently. 'It's amazing what a good sleep can do for you, isn't it?'

'Yes, it is, and it's amazing how seldom we get one,' Emma said with feeling. 'They'll be coming round with the breakfast trolley shortly. I suggest you try to eat something and . . . '

'*Breakfast?* You mean I slept all that time?'

'Yes.' Emma laughed. 'When I wasn't poking you and asking for your name, age and serial number.'

'Wow,' Cara murmured. 'Any news on the others?'

'Others? Oh, there's only you and Clive Ford still in hospital. And it's looking good for him, too. He was transferred to the spinal injuries unit, but they reckon once the swelling and bruising have gone down, he'll be fine. We sent everyone else on their way. You and Ray did a great job out there under very difficult circumstances.'

It all seemed like a dream now. Long ago and far away. And Greg Harding was part of the dream. Maybe she had dreamed him. Maybe she'd imagined him not once, but twice, carrying her to the bed . . . Her face burned.

'How is dear old Ray?' Emma went

on, snapping Cara out of her thoughts.

As Cara was about to answer, another doctor came over. He looked the sort who thought a lot of himself, Cara thought. She didn't like the way he just barged into the conversation between herself and Emma, as if being a patient she was of no consequence. It was rude, and if she'd been in Emma's shoes, she would have told him so.

'Where's Greg?' he demanded. 'I've been trying to get hold of him for the past hour. No one seems to know where he is.'

'That's because no one does,' Emma replied. 'He's taken leave owing him and is to be left in peace. I suggest if it's urgent, you speak to me. Greg won't be back for a fortnight.'

'Oh, for goodness' sake,' he said, exasperated, then he spun round and strode off.

Cara didn't know whether to be relieved or sorry that Greg wasn't planning to come back to the hospital. It meant she'd never see him again, and she knew she should be glad. Should be, but wasn't.

'Sorry about that,' Emma said. 'He can go jump if he thinks for one minute that I'll tell him where Greg is. The poor guy needed a good rest — and between us, Claire and I made sure that he got it. He hasn't had any time off at all for months.'

'Claire's his sister-in-law, right?'

'That's right. He crashed at her place last night. We cooked it up between us. I knew he'd go straight there when he got off the ship and I told Claire to keep him there. I think you'll like Claire. She's a terrific doctor and a really nice person when you get to know her.'

Emma glanced around, then asked, 'Do you mind?'

She indicated the bed.

'Not at all,' Cara said and Emma perched her bottom on the edge, holding her crutches between her knees.

'Thanks,' Emma said. 'I've been on

my crutches all night.' She laughed and Cara warmed to her even more than she already had. 'Where was I? Oh, yes, I was talking about Claire Harding. I've never known anyone so dedicated to their patients as she was. She never looked at them as being elderly or beyond hope. I mean, geriatrics isn't the most glamorous branch of medicine, is it?'

'So what went wrong?'

'Well, losing Brad in that awful accident,' Emma said. 'She's just never got over it. She rarely leaves the house and only if someone is with her. Even having that dear little boy didn't help. Don't get me wrong, she's a wonderful mother and he's as well looked after as any child you'll ever see, but she's turned herself into a virtual prisoner in her own home and in effect she's imprisoned Danny too. And Greg too, in a way. It's all very sad.'

Cara bit the inside of her mouth.

'The accident,' she ventured. 'Did it involve a helicopter?'

'Yes,' Emma said, shaking her head. 'And if someone hadn't crashed their car into Greg's and delayed him meeting the air ambulance, it would have been him who was killed instead of his brother. Greg arrived at the scene of the fire just as the helicopter was taking off. There was an explosion inside the factory and it destroyed the helicopter in the air.'

Cara's stomach knotted. No wonder Greg had been paranoid about the helicopter buzzing round the ship. He'd seen at first hand what could happen if something went wrong — and not only that, he'd witnessed the death of his brother. And how must he have felt coming out on a chopper to the Helena in the middle of the night in a raging storm, only to have such a lukewarm welcome from her?

'Poor guy then had to break the news to his brother's pregnant wife that she was a widow. She just fell apart. A month later she gave birth and at first she didn't show any interest in the baby, but Greg stepped in and took care of them both. Anyway, you can make your own mind up about Claire when you meet her,' Emma went on. 'She's a lovely person.'

'Oh, I'm unlikely to meet her,' Cara replied. 'As soon as I'm discharged, I'm going to book into a hotel. I'm not planning on sticking around. And you said Greg was on leave anyway, so . . . '

Emma gave her a stern look.

'You honestly think Greg's going to let you check in to some hotel?' she asked.

'Well I'm not staying here,' Cara pointed out.

'No, you're quite right, you're not. Greg's going to pick you up tomorrow morning. He's taking you home with him.'

Emma patted her hand, gathered up her crutches and got to her feet.

Cara couldn't answer. Why on earth did he want to take her home with him? He didn't even like her. And wasn't it rather high-handed of Greg to simply assume that she'd have nowhere else to go?

'Something wrong, Cara?' Emma asked, frowning. 'You don't look very pleased about that.'

Cara wanted to say that she wasn't pleased, but wouldn't that sound terribly ungrateful?

A little later one of the healthcare assistants brought her a flower arrangement in a basket very similar to the one she'd received on board the ship.

'The florist said to tell you there are two cards because they sent you some flowers on the ship and forgot to attach the card,' she said.

Cara tore the envelopes open. Well that solved that mystery. The flowers, both lots, had been from Greg.

What are you supposed to make of that then, Cara? she thought to herself.

She looked at them and smiled. All these years with no flowers, and someone sent her two lots in as many days.

★ ★ ★

Greg walked into the ward the following morning and stopped in his tracks. The bed he'd been told Cara occupied was empty and neatly made as if she was long gone. Surely she wouldn't have discharged herself — and if she had, surely someone would have let him know?

The thought that she might have gone, that he'd never see her again, filled him with something that came close to despair.

He stopped a passing HCA and asked, 'Dr Sanford?'

'She's in the day room,' she said with a smile. 'She got up, made her bed — I tell you, having a broken collar bone means nothing to that woman — then she went and made a cup of tea for herself and Mrs Ellington in the next bed. After that, she went down to physiotherapy to save the physio a trip up here to see her. It's a good thing she wasn't ordered to bed rest because it would have been a job to keep her there.'

'I can imagine.' Greg smiled, thinking it sounded typical of the Cara he was coming to know that she didn't wait for things to happen. If it was in her power, she made them happen. 'Thanks, Alison.'

'She's a sweetie, though,' Alison added. 'Disobedient in the nicest possible way. She was just the same yesterday, going round trying to help out where she could.'

Greg walked down to the day room and found Cara sitting quietly flicking through the pages of an old magazine. He halted in the doorway and stood looking at her for a moment. There was a brisk busyness about her page turning, as if she hated to be still. And she would be hating it, he knew that much.

She was looking at the pages, but not seeing, not reading — just looking as if she were miles away, lost in her thoughts. She was wearing a hospital gown which was much too big for her and her slender frame seemed lost in it.

She turned suddenly and looked up at him, giving a little start. She gave him a dazzling but uncertain smile.

'Thank you for the lovely flowers,' she said. 'Both lots.'

'That's all right,' he said, relieved. At least she wasn't going to chuck them at him. 'I hope you didn't mind, but people always say flowers are so cheering.'

'Mind?' She laughed softly. If only he knew. 'Of course not. They're beautiful.'

Her eye was slightly blackened and the bruise on her head had spread a little, but the swelling had gone and she looked a great deal better than she had the day before yesterday when he'd sent her here in the ambulance. It had taken every ounce of his willpower not to rush over to the hospital to see her, but now, looking at her in that hospital gown, he wished he'd at least thought to bring her some nightclothes.

He hadn't wanted to come before because he was meant to be on leave, and coming to visit her might be seen as interest of a different sort. Emma had already made suspicious noises during one of his frequent phone calls to check on her progress.

'How are you feeling?' he asked, coming into the room and sitting in the chair opposite.

'Fed up,' she confessed with a sigh.

'Well you need be fed up no longer,' he said. 'I've come to take you home with me. I'm sorry I didn't bring you any of your things before — it was thoughtless of me. But I've brought you what I thought you'd need for now.'

'Don't apologise. You've got other things to worry about.' She shifted in her chair and bit her lip. 'And actually, I wanted to talk to you about that,' she went on. 'About coming home with you. There's no need, honestly. It's very kind of you, but I can make my own arrangements.'

He looked across at her. He had no doubt she could make her own arrangements, but he couldn't bear the thought of her spending the next two weeks in some impersonal hotel among strangers. She needed looking after, pampering, and most of all she needed someone there to tell her to take things easy.

'It's no problem,' he said. He'd thought he'd probably have a fight on his hands, but looking at her now, he wondered if he'd overestimated her. She'd put on a show today of getting out of bed, getting on, keeping herself busy, but it was just a show. She looked exhausted and ready to admit to it. 'Let someone else take care of you for a change, Cara.'

'I don't need anyone to take care of me,' she said fiercely, despite the defeat in her eyes. 'I've always looked after myself. I see no reason for that to change just because I have a few aches and pains.'

But he wasn't going to back down, either.

'Just for tonight then,' he said. 'I've made up the spare bed for you. Besides, all your belongings are at my house. Oh — apart from this.'

He reached into the bag he'd brought with her clean clothes and pulled out the tatty old koala.

'I thought you might . . . ' he began, but her eyes had filled with tears at the sight of the old toy. He handed the koala to her and she took it wordlessly and clutched it against her cheek, her silent tears falling into the bitty brown fur.

Greg moved towards her, hunkering down in front of her, careful not to knock her knee. He wanted to gather her up in his arms, but there was nowhere he could touch her without causing pain. But she was already in pain. Something was hurting, something deep inside, and it was far more than disappointment over the cruise, or the discomfort of her injuries.

'Blast it,' he growled and gathered her against him anyway. She went limp in his arms, her tears soaking into his cotton shirt, her hair soft against his chin so that he had no choice but to kiss her head.

'Let's get you out of here, Cara. Let me take you home.'

This was more than the kind of sympathy hugs he administered to his sister-in-law. Much more. And the warm feel of her in his arms was almost more than he could stand.

⋆ ⋆ ⋆

He walked her back to her bed, swished the curtains shut around it and called a nurse to help her dress while he waited outside. He'd chosen clothes he thought she would find easy to get into. A loose white cotton shirt and a long cotton skirt with blue flowers, the same colour as her eyes.

When the nurse left, he went in and found Cara struggling to get her sandals on.

'Let me,' he said. 'There, that didn't hurt too much, did it?'

'Not at all,' she admitted.

He gazed into her eyes and she had to turn away in case he saw what must surely be naked in hers. She'd never been in this position before, the position of hiding her feelings. Never had to be.

'About earlier . . . ' she began.

'No need to explain,' he said. 'After all you've been through it would be surprising if you weren't a little upset.'

'A little upset? You're being kind, Greg. I was more than a little upset and quite disproportionately so. My tears had nothing to do with what happened on the ship,' she explained. 'It was seeing Snooky again. My koala.' She laughed softly and picked the toy up, holding it in her lap. 'This may sound crazy, but he's been around as long as I can remember. My granny gave him to me when I was very young. He's been everywhere with me and I guess I thought he'd been lost or forgotten. Until you got him out of the bag, I hadn't even realised. But it's pathetic, isn't it? To find myself so attached to a toy at my age?'

'Everyone needs a prop, Cara,' Greg said, offering her his arm so she could stand up. 'With some people it's cigarettes, others it's alcohol. So you chose an old bear, so what? At least it's healthy.'

Cara laughed and gave the koala a shake.

'I don't know about healthy,' she remarked. 'He's full of dust and probably a haven for all kinds of germs. And by the way, koalas aren't bears.'

'By the way,' he returned, his eyes sparkling, 'I know.'

As she stood Cara considered the effectiveness of modern pain relief and was thankful for it. She was perfectly capable of walking unaided, but when she tried to remove her hand from Greg's arm, he covered it with his free hand. It felt good to hold on, so she did.

'So what's your prop, Greg?'

'I don't need one,' he said and pulled the curtains open.

213

'You said everyone did,' she reminded him.

'Well, maybe.' He sighed, but he still didn't answer her question and Cara wondered whether somehow he had learned to use his grief as a crutch.

As they walked slowly down the ward, patients in the other beds called out.

'Goodbye, Cara! Good luck in your new job.'

'Take care, Cara! Thanks for the cocoa.'

Almost everyone in the ward had something to say to her. Greg was astounded. The HCA he'd spoken to earlier came over and kissed her cheek and one by one the rest of the nursing staff came to say goodbye. Cara asked them to pass her flowers on to a lonely old lady in the bed at the end of the ward and Greg nodded his approval.

'What are you, some kind of witch?' he whispered. 'You've been here less than two days and they're all sorry to see the back of you.'

'It's only male doctors that make lousy patients,' Cara said.

She felt ridiculously cheerful. Glad to be leaving hospital even after such a short stay, but even more so to be leaving with him. And the tears she'd shed had been cleansing somehow. She'd spent too much time thinking about the past lately and she'd needed that release.

Outside the sun was shining and the only indication that there had even been a storm was a scattering of leaves on the grass, ripped prematurely from the trees.

She got into the car and he fastened her seat belt, made sure she was comfortable, then hurried round to the driver's side. There was a child's car seat in the back and several colourful toys scattered on the seat.

'My nephew's,' he said when he got in and saw her looking at the baby paraphernalia. 'Danny. He's two.'

'He must spend a lot of time with

you to have so much stuff in your car,' she remarked.

'Not as much time as I'd like,' he admitted. 'How do you fancy going for a spin before I take you home?'

'Sounds good to me.'

Greg drove out of town and down leafy country lanes. Autumn was some way off yet, but already the trees were looking dark and tired, their leaves beginning to curl dryly in the heat. The road he took was little more than a car's width and grass sprouted down the centre.

'Where are we going?'

'You like horses?'

'I love horses.'

He turned off down a rutted track and pulled up outside some farm buildings next to other parked vehicles. Cara could see horses grazing in the fields and the whole scene looked so peaceful, she let out a deep contented sigh.

Before she could get out of the car, Greg was opening the door for her. She paused to lean on the fence and drink in the view. One minute they had been driving through a quite densely wooded area and now they were here, where fields rolled into the distance, broken up by uneven hedgerows.

'It's beautiful,' she whispered.

'Dr Harding! You made it.'

Cara turned to see a man hurrying towards them. He grasped Greg's hand and shook it warmly, then he turned and beamed at Cara.

'Hi, Harry,' Greg said. 'This is . . . '

'Cara,' Cara said quickly, seeing no reason to stick to formalities. 'Hi. Pleased to meet you.'

'Harry's daughter, Chloe, was a patient of mine,' Greg explained as they followed him across to the paddock where a small girl was sitting astride a pony. As soon as the child saw Greg, she began to wave furiously.

'Doctor Greg!' she called. 'Look at me.'

'I am looking at you, sweetheart,' he replied. 'How did you get all the way up there? Did you have to use a ladder?'

'No, silly.' She giggled. 'It was easy. I can climb up and down myself. And Heather is so gentle. Come and speak to her.'

Greg and Cara walked over, but it was Cara the pony nuzzled. What was it about her, Greg wondered, that made people and animals instantly like her? But not him.

Except he wasn't even kidding himself any more. The very reason he'd been so chilly with her was because he knew deep down he was attracted to her and sensed the danger of it.

'She's absolutely beautiful,' Cara said. 'Does she belong to you, Chloe?'

'No,' Chloe said. 'But I come to ride her twice a week.'

'Dartmoors are wonderful ponies for kids,' Greg commented. 'Gentle-natured, kind-hearted.'

'Therapeutic,' Cara murmured under her breath as she gave the placid pony a last stroke before the riding instructor in the paddock called Chloe over. The child turned the pony with ease and trotted gently across.

'Excuse me, Dr Harding,' a woman said. 'You won't remember me, I'm . . . '

'Sally,' he answered. 'Chloe's mum. How are you?'

She blushed. 'Me? Oh! I'm fine, thank you. But what do you think of our girl? It's thanks to you that she's here at all.'

Cara heard Harry telling one of the stable hands that Greg was the doctor who had saved his little girl. For a moment she considered whether this was why he'd come, to lap up the praise, but an instant later she changed her mind and realised she'd done him a massive disservice. He wasn't listening. His eyes were on the child, watching her every movement. His interest and his affection were genuine.

He didn't take his eyes off Chloe in all the time they watched her putting the pony through her paces.

'Marvellous,' he declared. 'She's a natural in the saddle.'

When she'd finished, he was the first one to clap and then everyone else joined in, including Cara.

'That was fantastic, Chloe,' he cheered.

'Thank you so much for coming,' Sally said. 'It means a lot to us that you came. When Harry said he'd asked you, I didn't think you'd be able to make it.'

Cara drifted away to where she had stood when they first arrived. She hadn't ridden a horse for years. In fact when she thought about it, she hadn't done anything for herself. Looking back over the years since she went to university, all she had done was work. She'd lived it, breathed it and it left no time for anything else.

As for her home — it wasn't a home. Not in the true sense of the word. It was a place to sleep and occasionally eat and she'd put about as much thought into her new home as she did into what brand of washing powder to buy. She couldn't even remember the layout of her new place. All she knew was that it had a functional kitchen, tv small bedrooms and a lounge room tha overlooked a small back yard. It was set among other identical, equally functional buildings, mainly occupied by hospital staff since it was only a ten-minute drive from the hospital where she was to take up her new post.

There was a spare bedroom, which would only be used if she had any colleagues on placement to stay over with her. And on the rare occasions that had happened, she normally left them to their own devices. She'd made a few lasting friendships that way, but even those she considered her closest friends didn't know the real Cara Sanford.

Her father was no longer in touch and Cara realised with a jolt that if she'd died on that cruise ship, it wouldn't have made a lot of difference to the lives of anyone else.

As a child, riding had been her only escape from the misery at home. On the back of a pony she had been able to forget everything. Why on earth had she ven it up? She frowned and it dawned on her that since her mother died, she'd given up everything and anything that brought her pleasure.

The sound of clopping hooves startled her and she turned to see a very small child sitting astride a Shetland pony, being led along by a pretty young girl. The child called out to Cara and waved as she was led past.

Cara waved back. She hadn't realised that the riding school was also used as a therapy centre for special needs children. It was a wonderful idea and had probably helped young Chloe recover from her injuries. The movement and warmth of a horse provided a whole range of benefits for its rider. And it wasn't something that only benefited those with physical disabilities.

* * *

Cara was leaning on the fence, deep in thought when Greg found her. She looked so right in this setting with a warm breeze ruffling her hair, rippling the soft fabric of her shirt and wafting the hem of her long skirt. Despite the earthy aroma of a distant ploughed field drifting in, the air felt clean and fresh in a completely different way to the freshness of the air by the sea.

She was a chameleon. She'd looked great in sports gear, at home in smarter clothes — she'd even looked good in a shapeless hospital gown!

'I'm sorry,' he said. 'You must be tired. I shouldn't have left you hanging around.'

But when she looked up at him, her face was alight. He'd thought her dazzling that day on the dock, but the glow on her face and the brightness of her eyes outshone even that.

'Cara,' he breathed. 'What's happened?'

'Greg,' she said. 'Does Claire ride?'

'Claire?' He shook his head, puzzled as to why she should ask, why she should even be thinking about his sister-in-law. 'I doubt it. City born and bred, was our Claire.'

'Do you think she'd like to?'

He frowned, then led by the smile on her face and her dancing eyes, he began to see what she was getting at.

'It's not something I've ever considered,' he admitted. 'It would do Danny good to learn to ride, too. Thanks for suggesting it, Cara. Now, are you ready to leave?'

He offered his arm with a grin and she took it. For once, the mention of his sister-in-law's name hadn't filled him with hopelessness. This time he felt something else — and it felt very much like hope.

'Claire's already taking steps to improve things,' he explained as they walked to the car. 'She walked to the shop on her own which may not sound much, but it's a giant leap for someone who hasn't left the house on her own for two years.'

'Greg, had you ever considered that Claire may have been suffering from postnatal depression? It could have been mistaken for grief, masked by her already present unhappiness.'

Greg stopped in his tracks.

'Sometimes — ' she rushed on. 'Sometimes, we can be too close to someone, to a situation, to see what's obvious.'

She didn't even know Claire, didn't know the circumstances, how could she possibly make a sweeping statement like that? Did she really think that he didn't know the difference between grief and postnatal depression?

'Cara, I don't . . . '

'My mother,' she continued, licking her lips, a deep frown creasing her forehead. 'My mother died because . . . because everyone thought she was simply miserable and upset about my father walking out on her. I was the one person who should have seen that she was dying. She died of a broken heart, Greg, but she didn't have to. If I'd sought proper medical help instead of thinking that my love alone could bring her back from the abyss, then maybe, just maybe, she'd be alive today.'

Breathless after her speech, Cara took stock. There. She'd never said it out loud before — much less admitted to herself that she harboured such guilt.

'Your father walked out on her?'

'After making her life a living hell for years, yes,' Cara said, her voice acid. 'After making her give up her dreams, her career, everything she cared about, yes, he walked out on her. He walked out on both of us.'

She shook herself and her smile was back. The armoured smile with which he'd noticed she tried to protect herself.

'But this is such a glorious day, Greg, and it's so peaceful here. Don't let's spoil the mood. Can we go somewhere and have a picnic lunch?'

'Yes, why not?' he said, his voice hoarse. 'There's a bakery in the village that sells rolls. We'll swing by there and pick something up.'

* * *

Greg parked in the shade of the trees growing around the church and left Cara in the car while he crossed the road to the bakery. As he walked in, the smell of fresh bread made him realise just how hungry he was. He hadn't eaten breakfast this morning. In truth, he'd been too nervous to stomach more than a cup of coffee.

What madness had made him want to bring Cara into his home was beyond his comprehension. No matter how much he told himself he was doing a good deed, he had to wonder at his motives. He didn't want her staying in a hotel because he cared about her.

But what use was caring about someone who was about to go back to the other side of the world? If it wasn't for Claire and Danny, he might even have considered uprooting himself and following her, just to see where it took him, just to see if he could get to know the real Cara Sanford.

He wasn't going to walk out on Danny. Even if things were okay with

Claire, if she had no problems at all, Danny still needed a father figure in his life; someone to ride him on his shoulders and do all the things Brad would have done.

He ordered rolls and picked up a couple of cans of cola from the shelf. This wasn't really his idea of a perfect picnic. Perfect would be cooked chicken, potato salad, crispy rolls, strawberries and a bottle of light sparkling wine.

He paid, left the shop and as he waited to cross the road, he looked at Cara sitting in the passenger seat, head back, eyes closed. He'd known there was something special about her from the first moment he set eyes on her on the dock. It felt like a lifetime ago, yet it was mere days. He felt as if he'd known her forever . . . although he knew so little about her.

Was this purely physical? He couldn't deny the effect she had on him. When he'd been tending her injuries on board the ship, he'd had some very unethical thoughts about her. But did she feel the same way?

The road was empty, but he remained where he was, waiting to cross. As if she'd sensed his eyes on her, Cara turned to look at him and then she smiled. He took a step forward and there was a deafening whoosh and the blast of a horn. Greg leapt back as a lorry thundered past.

'Good grief,' he whispered. 'Where did that come from?'

When he looked across the road again, Cara was out of the car, concern etched into every line of her face.

He laughed and shrugged, feeling like an idiot. And on her face, concern turned to relief and she was laughing too.

11

The sun had dried the grass on the river bank, but Greg put a blanket down on the ground before Cara sat down, which she did with remarkable grace considering her discomfort.

'It's lovely here,' she remarked. 'So peaceful, so quiet.'

Weeping willows draped their fragile-looking boughs in the water where ducks swam lazily. A family of swans came towards them, the parents pristine white, their cygnets still brown, but grown big over the summer. A squirrel pranced up the trunk of an oak tree and watched them from one of the lower branches.

'I feel as if I'm in a Disney movie.' Cara sighed. 'It's so idyllic here. I almost expect the animals to start talking to us.'

'They are, in their way,' Greg pointed

out, leaning back on his elbows. 'They're all asking us to save them a few crumbs.'

Cara moved into a comfortable position, flat on her back staring up at the sky. It looked superb, that late summer sky, blue and clear with a few wispy white clouds floating up high.

'We don't take the time to look up at the sky often enough,' she mused. 'When was the last time you looked at the sky, Greg? I mean, really studied it?'

She felt him move beside her, felt the warmth of his body touching hers as he lay next to her on the blanket. And she liked the feel of his body next to hers — very much.

'Too long ago,' he admitted.

'Listen,' she murmured, closing her eyes. 'You think it's so quiet and yet if you listen, there's so much going on.'

She was talking about the bees buzzing, the trickle of water, birds singing, leaves rustling. She felt Greg move again, and thought perhaps he'd moved away.

Would he have invited her to stay in his home if he knew how much she liked him? Liked! That had to be the understatement of the decade — the century! She felt her heartbeat quicken, imagined what it would be like to kiss him, to have him kiss her. Her lips parted involuntarily and she let out the softest of sighs.

She could almost imagine the warmth of his breath on her cheek, feel the closeness of him . . . and then she wasn't imagining any longer. The breath was real, the closeness was real and his lips on hers were all too real.

His hand cupped the back of her head, lifting her slightly, pressing his lips harder against hers.

Cara had been kissed before, but never like this.

He stopped, pulled away a little and brushed her hair back from her face, his eyes checking out every inch of her face as if he wanted to commit it all to his memory.

'Why . . . why did you do that?'

'Isn't it obvious? I've wanted to from the minute I first set eyes on you.'

'But I thought . . . I thought you didn't like me.'

'Does this convince you otherwise?' he asked and he kissed her again and this time it seemed to be deeper, harder.

When at last he pulled away, his eyes were smoky with desire. Cara's stomach swirled with feelings that she'd never felt before.

And if she let things progress, if she allowed him to possess her the way he wanted to and she wanted him to, what then? How could she go back to her lonely, solitary life in Australia? Because she knew that once she'd had a taste of the fruit she'd forbidden herself for so long, there would be no going back. She'd never settle. A cloud descended over her face and suddenly spots of rain began to fall.

'Quick,' Greg said, gathering up their picnic and helping her to her feet. 'We'll sit under the tree. It's dry there.'

'I didn't see that coming,' Cara said. She wasn't sure if she was referring to the rain clouds that had appeared from nowhere or to what had just happened between her and Greg.

The ground under the tree was dry and dusty. Greg put the blanket down again, then they sat down and ate the delicious chicken salad rolls. Afterwards Greg broke a little bread up and they walked down to the edge of the river and stood side by side to scatter it on the water for the grateful birds.

Cara held his hand. How was it possible that holding someone's hand could feel so right? The smell of the river, of damp earth and clean rain, filled her senses. She had never felt more alive than she did at this moment, never so aware of her own body, the rhythm of her heart, the soft catch of her breath.

The rain was fine and dampened her hair, making it darken and curl about her face and when she looked up at Greg, he kissed her again. Then he looked at her in wonder as if he, too, thought he was dreaming.

* * *

What on earth was he thinking? Kissing her like that! But there was no power on earth that could have stopped him. Cara's mouth had looked so inviting, and he'd never been one to turn down an invitation. And the rebuke he'd expected never came. She returned his kiss as hungrily as he offered it.

It was a kiss, that was all. And if he really thought that was all, then he was seriously kidding himself. Now here they stood in the rain, slowly getting soaked to the skin, watching as ducks and swans and a few shy moorhens and white-faced coots converged on the bread they'd thrown onto the water.

What kind of fool was he? He'd kidded himself he could take her into his home, look after her for a couple of weeks, then wave her off at some impersonal airport forever. He already knew that wasn't going to be possible. He didn't know how he was going to stop her leaving England, but he knew he had to find a way. For the first time in two years, he felt alive. He felt that life might just be worth living.

'You're getting soaked,' he said. 'We should head back.'

'I know,' she murmured, but she didn't move.

'Really,' he said, putting his arm around her.

She looked up at him and the look she gave him nearly blew him away. How could a woman of her age, with her experience and her skill, look so scared and innocent and so totally and utterly vulnerable?

★ ★ ★

'What a lovely house,' Cara said as he pulled up on the drive. It was, too. Very attractive with dark red bricks and leaded windows. It was a house with

236

character — unlike the cold, functional places she had always called home.

'It suits me,' he said.

'It's a family house. Does Claire live with you?'

'God! No,' he answered.

And what did that mean? From the very start, she'd wondered about his relationship with his sister-in-law. Just how close were they? Very, from what Emma had said.

'You'd better have a bath and get into some dry clothes,' he said as he opened the wide oak front door into the hall. 'I'll get some towels. Would you like a hand getting up the stairs?'

'No, I'll be fine. You don't have to mother me, Greg.'

'Maybe I like taking care of you.'

'Maybe I'm not used to it.'

At the top of the stairs, he showed her into a large bedroom with a window overlooking the huge garden and school fields at the rear of the house. He pushed open another door into the adjoining bathroom.

'Do you need help removing the bandages?'

'I can manage — thanks.'

'Of course,' he said raggedly.

'And I think I'll use the shower rather than the bath.'

He slid open the glass door to the shower cubicle and turned on the water, testing it until it felt right.

'That feels fine, Cara. I'll be in my room across the hall. When you're ready, sing out. I don't think it's a good idea for me to stay in here, do you?'

'Probably not,' she said huskily. 'Thanks, Greg.'

She was thanking him for more than the shower. She was thanking him for not trying to take things further — but at the same time, she felt disappointed that he hadn't.

★　★　★

Without the support of the bandages, Cara had to take care to keep her shoulders up straight. There was a slight bump over the site of the break, but it was small and she knew with care it would heal quickly. She dropped the towel and stepped into the shower cubicle. The water was pleasantly hot and soothing.

Greg was right. If she had gone to stay in a hotel, she wouldn't have managed very well on her own. She would have had to visit an outpatient clinic every day to have the splint tightened, and dressing herself would have been a problem.

For the moment, she needed him. And in two weeks she would be on her way home, geared up and ready for the challenge of her new job.

As the water struck her body like hot needles, she thought about going home. Why wasn't she looking forward to it as much as she had been? And what was the alternative? To give it all up, throw everything she'd worked so hard for away . . . for a man? She almost laughed out loud.

She turned the water off, stepped out

and picked up the towel, arranging it around her as best she could before calling Greg. He was there in an instant with more towels and a fresh set of bandages.

*   *   *

Cara sat on a chair in the steamy bathroom while he dried her back, then he set to work splinting her shoulders. She had a very straight back and a neat hollow over her spine. He wanted to run his finger down the line of her spine, but he resisted.

The phone rang.

'Blast,' he cursed. 'They'll have to wait. I'm not going to leave you sitting there like that.'

'It might be important,' she protested. 'You should never ignore a ringing phone.'

'This is more important,' he said. 'You're more important.'

He got on with bandaging her once more in a figure of eight, strapping her

240

up firmly, making sure it was comfortable.

'That feels so good,' she said. 'The doctor who tightened it at the hospital this morning didn't do it as firmly as that.'

'It isn't too tight?' he asked.

'It's perfect.'

The phone began to ring again. This time he hurried across to his room to answer it.

He returned few minutes later, a thoughtful look on his face.

'How would you like to meet Claire and Danny?' he asked.

'Now?'

'Yes, if you're feeling up to it.'

'Sure,' she said. 'That was Claire on the phone?'

'It was. She's been talking to Emma. I warn you, Cara, those two have had their heads together over us and . . . '

'Us?'

'For some reason, Emma thinks you and I would make a good couple,' he said, grinning.

'Wonder what gives her that idea.' Cara laughed, but she felt nervous about meeting Claire all the same.

'What should I wear?'

'Something comfortable,' he answered.

'How about jeans and my blue check shirt? Would that do?'

He found them in her suitcase and put them out for her and once again left her to it. When he came back, she'd managed to dress herself. The jeans were tight and hugged her hips and thighs. She looked better than good. They clung to every curve, yet sat neatly on her hips without digging in. But the collar of her shirt was caught up. As he reached to straighten the collar, she turned her head and kissed his hand.

A spontaneous gesture of affection. She'd never done anything like that before. Ever. It shocked her.

She blushed. If only she were fifteen years younger! Young people seemed so much more at ease with themselves.

'Something wrong?' Greg asked.

'No.' She shook her head. 'I was just getting a bit ahead of myself. Worrying about things that might never happen.'

'Please don't worry about meeting Claire,' he said, misunderstanding her meaning. 'You'll love her and she'll love you — but if you're too tired, I can call her back and cancel.'

'No, I'll be fine. I'd like to meet her. And Danny.'

★ ★ ★

The front door of the square, modern house opened and a small boy raced out. He wore red bibbed shorts and a red check shirt. He pulled up just short of Greg and Cara and stared up at Cara, his thumb flying to his mouth. What a gorgeous little boy, with a pixie face and eyes that positively shone with mischief.

'Who's that?' he murmured round his thumb.

'It's Uncle Greg's friend, Cara,' said the woman who had followed the child outside, with a smile. 'Take your thumb out of your mouth and say hi.'

This must be Claire. She wasn't quite as Cara had expected, although she couldn't say exactly what she had expected. Claire was small and neat with hair almost as dark as Greg's, and soft grey eyes. She was slim — possibly too slim.

Danny removed his thumb and grinned, showing neat rows of small white teeth.

'Hi, Cara.'

'Hi, Danny,' she answered.

His attention was completely on her.

'Hey, don't I get a hug?' Greg asked and Danny swung his hips from side to side, a shy smile stealing over his face. He wasn't hugging anyone in front of this new person! He took a couple of steps towards Cara, then pulled his thumb from his mouth and offered her his soggy hand.

She took the tiny hand in hers. Wonderful how such a little person could make you feel so welcome.

'Come in,' Claire urged. 'The sun's on the back of the house and it's lovely out in the garden.'

The garden was compact, the grass threadbare. It must have taken a battering from Danny's small feet over the course of the summer. They sat on plastic chairs on a decking area while Claire went to collect a jug of iced lemonade from the kitchen.

Danny tore round the garden, arms outstretched.

Cara watched him.

'What do you think?'

'I think he's gorgeous. But he reminds me of one of those poor animals you see in zoos. The ones that pace round in circles or walk up and down endlessly. Is he always like this?'

'Most of the time, yes,' Greg admitted. 'I try to get him away from here as often as I can, but . . . '

Claire came out then and Greg looked away, guilt written all over his face. Cara guessed he'd never spoken so frankly to anyone before.

'So how are you feeling, Cara?' Claire asked. 'I heard you took quite a battering on that ship. You wouldn't catch me on a boat. I like to feel dry land under my feet.'

She talked nineteen to the dozen, the way isolated people often do when they suddenly find themselves with company. *She's even more nervous than I am*, Cara thought. She glanced at Greg and saw he was watching Danny running in circles, his jaw twitching. Suddenly he sprang to his feet.

'I'm going to take Danny to the park. Is that okay, Claire?'

'Well, yes, if you're sure you want to.'

'Yes, I want to,' he said firmly. 'We won't be long. I'll take a ball and we can have a kick around. Come on, Munchkin, let's go for a walk.'

Danny let out a squeal of delight and rushed to Greg's side, gazing up at him adoringly, like a dog about to be released from a cage.

He took Danny inside, washed his face and hands, picked up a ball and left Cara and Claire alone.

'He's great with Danny,' Claire said when Danny's gleeful chatter had faded into the distance.

'So I see,' Cara agreed. 'It must be difficult for you.'

'Difficult?'

'Being on your own,' Cara said.

'I'm not on my own,' Claire said. 'I have Danny — and Greg.'

'And friends too,' Cara added for her. 'I met Emma at the hospital. She's lovely.'

'Emma.' The tension faded from Claire's face. 'Yes, she's a very close friend. I have a lot of friends who call in to see me. I'm very lucky, really.'

They talked a little about Claire's friends from the hospital and she even touched on her work there in years gone by. Touched on it with a rather wistful air, Cara thought.

'How about Danny?' Cara asked. 'Does he have friends?'

Claire looked away, then began to fiddle with the jug, splashing more lemonade into their glasses.

'I was an only child,' Cara said. 'It was very lonely at times. I didn't have friends round often because my mum wasn't well.'

It had got too awkward. Friends came round, saw Cara's mother sitting at the table in her dressing gown at four o'clock in the afternoon and it freaked them out, especially when she wouldn't speak to them and appeared not even to see them.

She looked across at Claire, half expecting her to bristle, but she didn't. Claire was a long way from the all-day dressing gown and uncombed hair.

'How did you cope?'

'Very well really,' Cara said. 'Kids are expert at adapting. They take what life deals them and they handle it. But going riding helped. It helped a lot.'

'Horse riding, you mean?'

'Yeah.' Cara smiled. 'I used to ride a dappled grey pony called Princess. Corny, huh? She was so quiet and gentle. I used to talk to her, tell her all my problems and she always listened. So hey, now you know I'm crazy.'

Claire looked thoughtful. 'I had a dog when I was a kid,' she said, her eyes softening. 'A collie called Trixie. I've always thought I'd like another dog one day.'

'But not a pony?' Cara grinned.

'Does it look as if I have room for a pony?' Claire spread out her hands towards her small garden and laughed. 'Seriously, I've only even ridden at fêtes. You know the kind of thing, fifteen minutes, once round the ring for a pound. I liked it, though.'

'It's never too late to learn,' Cara urged. 'Greg and I stopped by a stable today to see an ex-patient of his riding a pony. They take very young children. And I bet they'd teach adults too.'

Claire seemed to retract, like a startled turtle slipping back into its shell, and Cara realised she'd put her toe just a mite too far across the line.

Claire got to her feet and began to

slam the jug and glasses back on the tray. Her hands were shaking. Cara also stood. She was quite a bit taller than Claire, which made her feel awkward and gawky.

'I'm sorry,' she offered. 'I didn't mean . . . '

'I know you didn't,' Claire said. 'I'm not angry with you. I'm angry with myself. It's as if these past few weeks I've started coming to my senses, do you know what I mean? I've been taking a long, hard look at myself and I don't much like what I see. I walked to the farm shop on my own and I was so pleased with myself, as if I'd climbed a mountain. Just how pathetic is that? I never used to be so dependent. Before Brad was killed, we lived very independent lives.'

'Recognising that you have a problem is the first step towards solving it,' Cara said gently. 'And Greg says you are a wonderful doctor.'

'Yes,' Claire answered. 'I was.'

'No, you are,' Cara corrected. 'Who

you are and what you are hasn't changed.'

'Hasn't it?'

'No, of course not.'

Claire set the tray back down. 'We used to have a goldfish. Well, Danny did. We kept it in a tank in the kitchen. I used to watch it swimming up and down, up and down behind the glass, staring out at the same old view hour after hour, day after day. I felt sorry for that fish. It seemed such a sad, empty life and eventually I asked Harold next door if we could release it into his pond. He agreed. I felt so good when I let that fish go, Cara. And then a few days later, Harold came round to tell me that a heron had been down and taken it from the pond. My fish.'

She pushed her fist against her mouth, tried to bite back the tears, but they were filling her eyes, spilling onto her cheeks.

'See what happens when you let the outside world in? Danny might be trapped here, but he's safe. And yes, I know I can't keep him here forever and I know he has to learn to mix in the wider world and I'm doing everything I can to get there, but . . . '

The gate opened and Greg appeared with Danny sitting on his shoulders.

★ ★ ★

They were both covered in mud, their faces red from exertion. Greg stopped in his tracks, his face like thunder as he slipped Danny down, placing him carefully on the ground.

He took in Claire's tear-sodden face, her fist pressed against her mouth and then he looked at Cara. His eyes were so cold. Cara almost expected to freeze where she stood, to find herself encased in a block of ice.

Claire spun round, fished a tissue from her pocket and dabbed at her tears.

Cara put a hand on her shoulder.

'It's all right, Claire,' she whispered.

Claire nodded imperceptibly, then

252

she turned round a beaming smile plastered on her face.

'Oh, my,' she said. 'Danny you're filthy! You need a bath right now. What mischief has Uncle Greg got you in this time?'

Danny ran squealing past her into the house as fast as his little legs could carry him.

'Excuse me, won't you,' Claire said to Cara. 'Perhaps you'd like to call again sometime. Thanks for coming round. Thanks for taking him out, Greg.'

She smiled briefly, then turned on her heel and rushed into the house behind her son.

★   ★   ★

'What the hell did you say to her?' Greg blazed furiously once they were in the car.

'Say? I didn't . . . '

'She was in floods of tears when we came back. Did you think I wouldn't notice?'

253

'We had a long talk,' Cara began to explain, hurt by his anger, hurt even more that he was willing to think so badly of her without hearing her explanation.

'I bet,' he growled. 'What did you talk about? Her depression? I heard her trying to explain herself to you.'

'It wasn't like that.'

'Wasn't it?'

'Fine!' Cara snapped. 'You think it was wrong that Claire was explaining herself to me — well, I have no intention of explaining myself to you. You can go to hell as far as I'm concerned. You're obviously willing to think the worst of me. Well, go on then! Think what you damn well like.'

He gunned the engine and screeched off the drive. They didn't speak all the way back to his house and when they arrived, he marched round the car and flung open her door.

Cara's knees shook as she got out. She was so angry. For two pins and with one or two uninjured joints, she'd give him a good solid kick up the backside. But she was incapable.

He opened the front door, then stood back, ever the gentleman even if he had behaved like an absolute pig. She stepped past him into the hall.

'What would you like to eat?' he asked, his voice brittle.

'I'm not hungry.'

'Don't be stupid, Cara,' he protested, his voice mellowing. 'You have to eat.'

'Don't call me stupid. I meant what I said. I'm not hungry.'

'I'm sorry,' he said. 'You're not stupid. Let me make you something. An omelette? Some pasta? There's a good takeaway just up the road.'

'Good for them,' she said, wondering if they did Japanese tempura prawns and pineapple rice because she realised she was ravenous.

'Have a drink at least. Coffee?'

If her shoulders hadn't been strapped up so firmly, they would have slumped.

'All right,' she said.

'And then we'll talk about food.'

He pushed open the door to the lounge and she stepped in. The room was cool and comfortable. She went to a leather armchair by the window and let it swallow her up, kicking off her shoes, curling her legs up, hugging her knees. It felt comfortable to sit that way. Comforting.

Greg looked down at her.

'You shouldn't sit like that. Your knee . . . '

'Telling me how I should sit now, Doctor?' she said.

'You know what?' he snapped, anger rising again, turning his eyes to flashing green fire. 'You're impossible!'

And then he turned on his heel and marched through to his kitchen where he began clattering cups and pots.

Impossible. That just about summed up their situation.

12

The coffee was welcome. Cara put extra brown sugar in hers and stirred, then realised Greg was watching her.

'I'm sorry,' he said. 'I shouldn't have gone off at you like that. You didn't deserve it.'

'How do you know? You think I upset Claire.'

'She's easily upset.'

'She's a lot stronger than you're giving her credit for,' Cara said, knowing that his wish to protect his sister-in-law stemmed from love. She admired him for that, but a time would come when he'd have to step back and take stock. 'I mentioned the horse riding to her. She seemed quite interested.'

He shook his head. 'You're a fast worker. And something of an enigma. I've never met anyone quite like you,

Cara. You're just about the coolest, most efficient woman I've ever known, and yet there's a part of you that doesn't fit. There's a part of you that you're too frightened to let show, as if you've got a scared little girl hiding away in there somewhere.'

'Maybe I have,' she said flippantly, despite the thundering of her heart behind her damaged ribs.

'Don't go back,' he said suddenly, looking her straight in the eye. 'Stay here. See what happens.'

She laughed incredulously. 'You're asking me to give up my job, my whole life's work, for someone I've known less than a week? Come on, Greg, get real. I've worked too hard and too long for this. I'm not throwing it away for you or anyone else.'

She knew she sounded harsh, but she couldn't help herself. She didn't suppose her mother threw everything away on a whim. She must have thought she was deeply in love — must have thought Cara's father loved her.

She narrowed her eyes. 'If you want me so much, Greg,' she challenged, 'come back with me.'

'To Australia?'

'Why not? You're asking me to give up everything, now I'm asking you.'

'You know I can't do that,' he answered sadly. 'There isn't just me to consider.'

'And you think I don't have other considerations? You don't think I have friends, family, people who will miss me?'

She didn't, but he wasn't to know that. The truth was that no one in the world really cared about Cara — and up until now, that was how she liked it.

'I'm not thinking straight,' he said apologetically. 'I don't think I've been able to since the first moment I set eyes on you. I'm sorry, Cara. I should never have asked you to even consider it. Forget I said anything. It was totally stupid of me.'

'You're not stupid,' she said with a smile.

If it wasn't for her history, Cara wouldn't have even had to think about it. She would have taken the risk, dropped her plans and stayed with Greg, just to see what would happen.

'So what are we going to eat?' she asked. 'I'm starving.'

He went to the kitchen, pulled some takeaway menus from the corkboard and handed them to her.

'Take your pick,' he said.

'Chinese,' she said, pulling out one of the menus and discarding the rest. She flipped it open and licked her lips. 'Ooh, kung pao prawns . . . '

Half an hour later, Greg came in with a white carrier bag holding several plastic containers. Cara helped to unpack, taking the lids off and setting the steaming containers on mats on the table.

'Never buy a takeaway when you're hungry,' he said ruefully. 'I've bought far too much.'

Cara giggled. 'When else would you buy a takeaway?' she said. 'You'd hardly buy one if you weren't hungry.'

'This is true.' He grinned and pulled a bottle of red wine from the cupboard. 'Australian shiraz. Now there's a coincidence. Is that okay?'

'I love Australian wine,' she said.

They ate too much, drank too much and laughed a lot. Greg watched her eat.

He knew he shouldn't even be entertaining the thoughts that were going through his mind.

After they'd eaten, they took the remainder of the wine and went to sit in the living room, content and happy once more.

* * *

Greg sat on the sofa and arranged himself so Cara could lean against him and put her feet up. The wine had relaxed her and brought a flush of roses to her cheeks and she felt soft, warm and pliable curled up against his body. He'd just about stopped kicking himself

261

for flying off the handle with her earlier. What an arrogant fool he'd sounded.

If life had taught him anything these past few years, it should be to live life for the moment, and he had every intention of doing that. If Cara wanted to go home, then he'd let her go with dignity. He had no intention of clutching her round the ankles so she had to drag him across the airport on his stomach. The thought of that made him laugh.

'What's so funny?' Cara asked. 'Come on, share the joke.'

'I was just thinking about the day you leave.'

'And it made you laugh? Boy, you must be really keen to see the back of me.'

'Actually I was visualising you trying to walk away with me clinging round your ankles,' he admitted.

She joined in the laughter. Humour had always been a shield and they were both using it now.

'I don't want it to be the end when

you go back. I don't want to wave you off at the airport knowing I'll never see you again.'

'Hey, this is getting kind of serious. Let's just forget about me going back and enjoy the moment.'

'You're right,' he conceded. But the good mood had gone. Darkness had closed in outside and the humour had been dampened by reality.

'You know, I'm really tired.' Cara yawned. 'I think I'll turn in.'

★ ★ ★

Upstairs, Greg closed the curtains.

'Can you manage to get undressed?' he asked.

'I'm not helpless, you know,' she retorted tartly.

He took her shortie pyjamas from her bag. Silver silk. The flimsy garments slid through his fingers as he tried to shake them out. How on earth were you supposed to put these on? Slippery, slidy ridiculous things.

He looked up and she was laughing at him.

'Perhaps I should just borrow some of yours,' she teased.

'I don't have any pyjamas,' he said.

'Oh!' She blushed.

'Don't worry. How difficult can it be to sort out a pair of pyjamas?' He laughed.

He finally got them straight and placed them neatly on the bed next to her.

'Are you . . . ?'

'Quite sure, thank you!'

'I don't know why you bother with these,' he said gruffly. 'You may as well not be wearing anything at all.'

He stepped outside the bedroom and after a few moments called out, 'I'm right here if you need me.'

'I won't,' she answered. 'Oow!'

'Cara?'

'I'm fine.'

He clenched his fists and fought back the urge to rush in and help her, then he heard her whimper with pain and

264

couldn't hold back any longer.

She was sitting on the bed in the pyjamas, her eyes closed, biting her lip against the pain.

'I did it,' she said huskily and he understood how important her independence was to her.

'Yes, love,' he said gruffly. 'Now let's get you into bed.'

He pulled back the covers and she held his arm.

'Thank you.'

'Stop thanking me,' he said and gave her such a fierce look that she shrank away from him.

'Don't be afraid, Cara.'

And then he kissed her.

'I want to make love to you,' he whispered. 'But I can't.'

'Why not?' she whispered back.

'Because I don't want to hurt your poor, battered body.'

'I know you won't hurt me, Greg,' she murmured, even while a voice deep inside was urging her to take care. 'I trust you.'

He lowered his head and kissed her and this time there was no going back.

* * *

In the middle of the night, Cara was wide awake.

'Greg,' she whispered huskily.

'Hmm?' he answered. He couldn't sleep either.

'I don't want to go back. I want to stay here with you.'

He sat up when she said that, propped himself up on his elbow and looked down at her.

'No,' he said firmly.

'What do you mean, no?'

She twisted round so violently that her upper body screeched with pain.

'You have to go back,' he said. 'Nothing has changed. A few hours ago you wouldn't even entertain the idea of staying on here. I don't want you to stay here for the wrong reasons. If you stay, it has to be because that's what you want. Really want. You have to be sure.'

They snuggled back down and her chest ached. Hot, salty tears slid silently down her face and soaked into her pillow.

She didn't know what to do. She'd never felt like this before and while she felt wonderful, she was very afraid of where it could all lead.

★   ★   ★

In the morning, he brought her breakfast in bed. Warm croissants with butter and jam and freshly ground coffee.

She devoured the food and thought she'd never had an appetite like this in her life!

Was this why her mother had given up everything? To feel like this? Was this what love was all about? She almost felt it was worth it. But what happened when the rejection came? How did you cope with that? Perhaps you didn't. Her mother hadn't. But who was to say Greg would ever reject her in the same way?

'You look deep in thought,' he observed. 'Regrets?'

'No,' she said quickly. 'And I meant what I said, about not wanting to go back,' she went on.

For wouldn't it be worth risking rejection if it meant a year, two years, ten years with this man?

As if on cue, the phone rang.

'That'll be Claire,' he said.

The call brought Cara to her senses. Could she cope being married to a man who was at the beck and call of another woman? A man who would run the moment that other woman crooked her finger? He went off to his bedroom to answer it.

When he came back he said, 'We've been invited to Claire's for lunch. That okay with you?'

'Yes,' she muttered, already sounding like a jealous lover, already wanting to keep him to herself. And just how practical would that be? Was it selfish of her to want him all to herself?

★   ★   ★

'Where's Danny?' Greg asked as he and Cara took the side gate into the back garden. They could hear him laughing, but there was no sign of him in the garden.

'Next door,' Claire explained. 'With Harold.'

She was setting a picnic lunch on a wooden table under the trees in the corner of the garden.

'I thought we'd eat al fresco,' she said. 'Make the most of what good weather we have left.'

'More fresh salad,' Greg commented. 'You've been shopping again?'

Claire smiled. 'We went out early this morning and stopped by the park on the way home, too,' she said proudly.

She looked at the food set out on the table and paused for a moment.

'Tomatoes,' she exclaimed. 'Won't be a moment.'

When she came back she was empty handed.

'I can't believe it, I forgot to get any,' she lamented, and suddenly her fragile new confidence looked likely to collapse.

'Isn't that always the way?' Cara said quickly. 'I always seem to forget something when I go shopping.'

'We can do without tomatoes, Claire,' Greg added.

'No we can't,' she said decisively. 'It isn't a proper salad without tomatoes.'

'I'll pop up the road and get some,' Greg offered. 'I won't be long. I may as well walk.'

He smiled at Cara before he left. A special smile. A secret smile. A smile that made her heart do strange things.

When he'd gone, Claire looked long and hard at Cara.

'You look different,' she said. 'Are you wearing make-up?'

'No,' Cara said. Was she that

270

transparent? Was it written all over her face that last night she had made love for the first time in her life?

'Perhaps you're just feeling much better,' Claire suggested. 'I'm glad to have this chance to talk to you on our own. I'm really sorry about yesterday and that's what this lunch is all about, really. I . . . '

'You don't have to apologise,' Cara interrupted, feeling awful because she had resented coming here so much, resented losing precious time alone with Greg when time was in such short supply.

'Oh, but I do. But the fact is, talking with you did me good. I actually slept properly last night for the first time in ages. And this morning, when I went to the farm shop, I picked up a few things for Harold next door. He's getting on a bit and it suddenly occurred to me that I can help other people.'

'Of course you can,' Cara agreed. 'That's what you do.'

'I know. But more than that. I want

to get back to work, Cara. I decided last night. Just a few hours at first, at least until Danny starts proper school. I want to start living again.'

'Oh, Claire,' Cara exclaimed, squeezing her hand. 'That is such good news.'

'And I thought about what you said about the horse riding and I thought, *why on earth not?* I could do with getting fit and I've been told it's quite a physical activity. And Danny could learn to ride, too. He loves horses.'

An anguished shout from next door's garden shattered the moment. It was Harold and he was calling out for help.

'Oh, don't say Danny's tripped him up,' Claire said, rising from her seat and heading towards a loose panel in the fence.

Cara followed, not expecting to be of any help, but there for moral support if nothing else. If the old boy had taken a tumble, Claire might welcome a spare pair of hands.

But as they squeezed through the loose panel, Claire let out a scream.

Harold was bending over his pond trying to drag something out. It looked like a bundle of old wet rags — a bundle of rags with blond hair streaked with green pond weed. Harold couldn't find the strength he needed and Danny's head went back under the water.

'Oh, no,' Cara whispered. 'No, not this.' Just how cruel could fate be to one family?

Claire had frozen to the spot, her pale hands clasped over her mouth, the word 'no' repeating itself over and over into her cupped hands.

The child was heavy with his waterlogged clothes and the old man was sobbing as his arthritic hands fought in vain to free him from the water. Cara dashed forward, gripped hold of Danny's shorts and hauled him out of the water, lifting him in her arms, ignoring the shrieking pain in her neck and chest as she laid him on the ground.

'Call an ambulance,' she shouted.

Then she turned her attention to Danny.

'Can you hear me, Danny? Open your eyes,' she called. No response. She hadn't really expected one, but she'd clung to a shred of hope that there might be. 'How long was he in the water for?'

'I don't know, I don't know,' Harold sobbed. 'I turned my back just for a second . . . I should have been watching him.'

Gently, Cara tilted Danny's head back. Then she checked his mouth for obstructions.

She lowered her head, listening for breath sounds, watching for the rise and fall of his chest. Nothing. Not a thing. *Oh please, not this.* His little hands were so cold. Little hands that may never again hold an adult's, pick up a toy or sift through the sand. Moving fast, she covered his mouth with her own, pinching his nose as she blew gently and watched for his chest to rise.

If only he wasn't so cold.

After two rescue breaths she checked his pulse. Nothing.

With the heel of her hand and keeping her arm straight, she began chest compressions.

'One, two, three, four, five,' she counted before giving another rescue breath. She was barely aware of the pain in her collar bone as she worked.

All she could think of was the lifeless child lying on the ground. She didn't stop to ask if an ambulance had been called. There was no time. She had to trust that either Harold or Claire had done as she asked.

Danny's colour didn't improve. He wasn't doing anything on his own.

'Come on, Danny,' she urged. 'Help me here, sweetheart. Come back to us. Don't leave us.'

Please God, she thought. *I'll go back to Australia. I'll leave these people to get on with their lives, but just let Danny live.*

Bargains. Desperate people always made bargains.

If he breathes, if he wakes up, if he recovers, I'll go away and leave these people to resume their lives, I promise.

Pain began to seep in at the corners of her awareness. She fought it back. Nothing must stop her, not even for a moment. She had to keep going, at least until the ambulance got here. She glanced up once and saw Claire on her knees next to Harold, who was sprawled on the ground.

The pause let in the pain, which had been almost unnoticeable but had now become nearly unbearable as she resumed the rescue breaths and the compressions.

The mother in Claire had been unable to help her child, but the doctor in her had rushed to the rescue of the old man. He was conscious, but clearly unwell and Claire was doing her best to make him comfortable.

She didn't know how long she'd been going when she sensed Claire beside her.

'Did you call an ambulance, Claire?'

'Yes,' she said, then gritting her teeth added, 'How is he?'

'I won't give up,' Cara muttered, ignoring the question.

'Neither will I,' Claire said. 'I lost my husband, I will not lose my son too. Please . . . let me.'

'Are you sure you can?'

'Yes,' Claire replied steadily.

Cara handed over, then looked at Harold. He was sitting up propped against a garden bench. He looked shocked, pale and frightened, but he was conscious.

Then suddenly the loose panel in the fence was thrown aside with a thunderous crash and Greg was hurtling across the garden. He took in the scene at a glance, Claire crouched over her lifeless child, the old man sitting as if he'd been thrown across the garden and Cara standing helplessly by.

'Danny,' he gasped. 'No, oh no . . . '

Cara stepped out of his way as he charged across.

He pulled Claire out of the way. 'I'll

take it from here,' he said. 'You must be exhausted.'

She didn't argue but seemed relieved that Greg had arrived to take over. If anyone could make everything right, bring Danny back to life, Greg could.

Greg looked huge bent over the child who looked so tiny. He was focusing all his attention on his hand, on moving Danny's little chest.

'One, two, three, four, five . . . '

And then lowering his head, sealing Danny's mouth with his, breathing life into his uncooperative lungs.

'He's got some colour,' Cara whispered. 'Greg, his colour — he has circulation . . . '

'I heard you,' he said and continued with the rescue breaths. Danny was still not breathing on his own but the chest compressions could stop.

Cara turned to look at Harold and gave him what she hoped was a reassuring smile. *He's taken a step towards life*, she wanted to say. *A big step*. But it was still early days. The poor old man would never forgive himself if Danny died, but children near ponds, particularly children of Danny's age who were likely to be curious, likely to lose balance and fall in, had to be supervised constantly.

Cara felt Claire's hand slide into hers and she squeezed it. Her eyes were wide, pleading, but she was calm and quiet.

Greg kept going and then Danny's little body convulsed and he choked, gagged, coughed and started to scream.

It was the most wonderful sound in the world and as Greg moved aside, Claire gathered her son up in her arms, warming him with her body.

'Thank you, thank you,' she kept saying over and over.

Cara felt as if the string that had been holding her upright had snapped and she almost fell. Relief flooded through her and pain followed close on its tail.

Greg wrapped his arms around Claire and Danny and the three of them were huddled together as sirens wailed in the distance. Cara looked on, feeling like an outsider, feeling that she really didn't belong here.

She turned away abruptly and went to check on Harold, who was crying again.

'He's going to be all right,' she told him with a smile. 'I think we all are.'

'It's my fault,' he lamented. 'All my fault. That poor little boy ... poor Claire ...'

'He's all right, Harold,' she repeated reassuringly. 'They're all going to be all right.'

'I'm going to fill the pond in,' he said. 'It could just as easily have been one of my grandchildren. Someone will take my fish, won't they?'

'I'm sure they will,' Cara soothed. 'I think you should go to the hospital too. You've had an awful shock.'

'Me? No, I'll be all right,' he said and held up his hand, wanting her to help him to his feet. Cara gritted her teeth and pulled him up.

'Is there someone you could call?

Someone to come over and be with you?'

'I'll call my daughter,' he said.

Cara had made a bargain. With God, with herself, with whoever. *Let him live and I'll go away.* She didn't belong here. But the trouble with that was that she didn't feel she belonged anywhere any more.

13

Greg took Cara back to his house while Claire went in the ambulance with Danny.

They hardly spoke for the whole journey, as if a chasm had opened up between them leaving a yawning gap. Greg was deep in thought, probably going over what had happened in his mind, and Cara didn't blame him. He'd almost lost his nephew. It was quite something to have to come to terms with.

'You don't have to take me home,' Cara ventured. 'I'd like to come to the hospital with you.'

'That's not a good idea,' he replied. 'You need to rest — and it'd get crowded with all of us there.'

Crowded. Yes. That was right. She was just part of a crowd. Not a part of the family. Not wanted.

'Will you at least let me know how he's doing?' Cara asked.

Greg nodded. 'Of course.'

They got out of the car and he left the engine running while he unlocked the front door.

He looked at her for a moment standing in the hallway. She looked kind of lost and bereft and a part of him wanted to stay with her, but he knew she'd understand him wanting to be with Danny right now. There'd be time later to talk.

She went into the house and sat down. The only photographs on display in Greg's living room were ones of Danny. He was Greg's world, and if he'd died today . . .

She sat in the chair as the minutes ticked past, the pain in her ribs and collar bone a constant reminder of what had happened. It was a long time before she realised she could smell the pond water on her clothes. It was in her hair, soaked through to her bandages. But the physical pain was nothing compared to the pain deep inside. What happened today had simply reinforced what she already knew. She didn't fit into Greg's life. Never would.

What a fool you are, Cara Sanford, she told herself as she eased to her feet and made for the stairs. *You knew what would happen if you gave yourself away, didn't you? You knew what the consequences would be. So what happens to you now?*

She squared her shoulders and winced.

You go home as planned, that's what you do. You go home, you move into your cold, characterless home and you get on with your life, just as you've always done. You coped with that before, you can cope with it again.

She climbed the stairs. Climbed being the operative word. Every step was a mammoth effort. Every step a pain.

Was this what it was like to grow old? Was this all she had to look forward to?

Work, followed by a lonely old age? And all this nonsense about protecting her heart — where had it got her?

Her heart wouldn't break, but it may well turn to stone. It had practically dried up anyway through lack of use.

Even as she thought it, she knew it wasn't true. She had the heart of a woman. And she was a woman, in every sense of the word now. Whole, complete, except for one thing — the man she loved and could never have.

Oh, yes, Cara, you love him. You knew you would love him from the moment you saw him, knew he would be special. And you played it like a fool.

Good old fate, eh? Stepped in, stirred her life up, messed with her destiny then chewed her up and spat her out.

Who would have thought this time last week that so much could have happened? If she'd thought ahead at all, then she'd only thought in terms of where the ship would be. Heading towards the Canary Islands by now, the fortunate islands where she was told they didn't have rain, just liquid sunshine.

She was on the landing. A bath would be good, but a shower would have to do. It took her an age to escape from the splint, to peel the supports from her knee and ankle, but once she was under the flowing water, it was worth it. Hot water brought relief from pain and washed the tears from her eyes.

* * *

Greg entered the room, and stood behind Claire, his hands resting on the back of her chair. Danny was sleeping now, his cheeks blooming with colour, his chest rising and falling with beautiful rhythm, just the way it should.

He'd been bathed, warmed up, given a cuddle and he was resting peacefully, blissfully unaware of the fright he'd given everyone. Greg had spoken to his colleagues and they'd assured him that Danny would be fine.

Claire was leaning forward, holding his tiny hand in hers. He looked so much more baby than little boy when he was asleep. So angelic and peaceful. And something had shifted in Claire, too. Despite what had happened, she seemed stronger.

'I'm going to come back, Greg,' she declared. 'I promised myself that if he lived, I'd stop hiding away. I want to show him the world. The world outside our back garden, anyway. Life's too short to hide away.'

Greg squeezed her shoulder. He didn't hold with making promises to either yourself or whatever deity you believed in, but he knew a lot of people did. Fate dealt you the cards and you did what you could with them.

'You don't have to,' he began.

'Yes, I do,' she replied. 'I'm ready for this. I'm ready to move on and you should be too. I just kept thinking that if he died, then what kind of life have I given him up to now?'

'A good life,' Greg protested. 'You've

given him love, you've nurtured him . . . '

'I've kept him a prisoner,' she interrupted. 'It doesn't matter how we pretty it up, you know and I know that he hasn't had a normal life up until now. I've got plans for us, Greg, for Danny and me. Big plans. We're going to learn to ride and I'm going to take him away on holiday.'

'I can . . . '

'No, just me and Danny. We have to learn to make it on our own because one day you're going to want a life of your own. You deserve that much. I lost my husband and you lost your brother, but Danny didn't lose anything, because you can't lose something you've never had.'

She looked up at him, her eyes pleading for understanding.

'I'm so grateful to you for getting us through these past two years. You've been great and we'll still want you around, but we're not your responsibility any more, Greg. I take that burden from you.'

She'd obviously given this a lot of thought. Greg wondered just how long it had been building up inside her before Danny's near-death released it.

'I should call Cara,' he said distractedly.

'Call her? You mean she isn't here?'

'I took her home,' he answered.

'Why?'

'Why? Leaving her alone after all she's been through! She must have been in agony after hauling Danny's dead weight out of the pond and then working on him for so long.'

'She did what?'

'She saved his life, Greg. While I was falling apart, unable to move, Cara saved him.'

He tried to imagine her doing that. Danny would have been no lightweight and the water wouldn't have wanted to give him up. And he could see her doing it — putting her own pain aside, the absolute professional in her acting on instinct regardless of her own comfort.

'Didn't you realise? I'd only just taken over from her when you turned up. She'd been working on him for ages. If it wasn't for her, he'd be dead, because I was absolutely useless at first.'

No wonder she'd been so quiet. So pale. But in his shock, his thoughts had been so filled with Danny, what might have happened, he'd failed to see what was happening.

Emma dashed in then.

'I've only just heard,' she gasped, rushing to the bed and looking at Danny. 'I just came on duty. How is he? Oh, bless him, you wouldn't think anything had happened.'

She came back round the bed and grabbed Claire's hand. 'And how about you? Are you okay? What a fright for you. For all of you.'

Greg was hardly listening. Danny would be all right now. He was in good hands. The signs were all good and pointing towards a complete recovery, and a child who would be none the worse for his ordeal. He may be a bit more careful around water from now on, but that was no bad thing.

And Claire had more or less told him he was free. Free to get on with his own life. He would never want to be free of Danny. Nothing would ever change or lessen the love he felt for that little boy, but without the weight of guilt life would be so different.

Meanwhile. Cara was at home, all alone, and she had been for hours.

'I should . . . ' he began.

'Go, Greg,' Claire urged. 'Go on, go. We'll be fine here. Give Cara my love and thank her for me. I'll thank her myself when I see her, but, you know.'

'I know,' he said.

'I'll keep an eye on them,' Emma promised. 'Not that they'll need it.'

He stooped over his nephew, planted a soft kiss on Danny's cheek, then with a last smile at his sister-in-law, rushed from the room.

* * *

Thank God for painkillers, Cara thought as she flopped back on to the bed. She'd have been right up the creek without a paddle without them. Right up the creek and in a lot of pain.

She'd placed Snooky, her faithful old koala, on the small bedside cabinet and she reached out for him. He smelled like Greg. Amazing as that seemed. It must have been from when he was in his pocket. She held him close, closed her eyes and pretended it was Greg lying next to her.

She wanted to cry, but her eyes were dry and burning. *No more tears*, she told herself. The only way to avoid pain was to simply stop feeling, to zip herself back up and shut out the world.

She stayed there for a while, but knew she would have to leave soon. She'd got her breath back, gained a second wind so to speak, and was ready to move on another step.

★　★　★

Greg rushed into the house, but as soon as he was inside he felt the emptiness of the place close in around him. She wasn't here. He threw open the doors to the downstairs rooms, but knew they'd be empty.

Upstairs it was the same. The bathroom was still a little steamy and she'd left her towels neatly folded on top of the linen box. Her bag had gone. She had gone. There was nothing left of her here; nothing at all, not even a note.

But he was wrong. She had left something behind. A bundle of soggy, stained bandages that reeked of pond water. She'd left them in the bin.

He whirled round. She'd left the house with no splint to support her shoulders. She must be in agony.

He raced back down the stairs and ran out into the street, knowing he wouldn't find her there, knowing that if she was still in the area, he would have seen her as he drove home. He stopped in the middle of the road looking first in one direction, then the other.

Defeated, he walked back to his house and sat down on the front steps. He hadn't felt this desolate since the moment he saw the helicopter blown to pieces. He never expected to feel anything this deeply again.

Two weeks. Less than two weeks. That's how long he had to find her. And she could be anywhere. He got to his feet and went inside, picking up the telephone directory from the hall table. Perhaps she'd used his phone to book a hotel. He lifted the receiver and pressed the redial button. After three rings, Claire's recorded voice answered. 'I'm sorry, I can't come to the phone at the moment . . .'

He replaced the receiver. She hadn't called either a taxi or a hotel from here. The last call had been made by him. So she must have left on foot. Walked to the bus stop down the road? Where on earth had she gone? She couldn't have vanished into thin air, but that seemed to be exactly what she'd done, covering her tracks so effectively that he hadn't a hope of finding her.

But she'd need treatment, and where would she go for that? To the hospital, of course.

He swiped up his keys and ran back out to his car, leaving his front door swinging open behind him. He didn't even think about the possibility of burglary. And if he did, even fleetingly, he didn't care. Possessions could be replaced, people couldn't. If he was quick, he could get there before her.

★ ★ ★

He ran into outpatients, past startled nurses and straight to the reception desk.

'Cara Sanford,' he gasped. 'Has she been in?'

'Dr Harding.' Jill smiled. 'Why yes, Dr Sanford has been in. She saw . . . '

'Is she still here?'

'No, she left a few minutes ago. It's a wonder you didn't pass her. She . . . '

He didn't give the receptionist the

chance to finish, but turned and ran back out of the hospital. The town bus came right into the hospital grounds and stopped directly opposite the entrance. He spun round and saw a bus pulling out of the exit lane into the building rush hour traffic.

She had to be on that bus. Where else would she be?

He raced back to his car, sped out of the car park and followed the bus into town. It was several vehicles ahead, but he kept it within his sight, carrying out risky manoeuvres at roundabouts and using the bus lane to get past the traffic.

Every time it stopped, he watched the passengers getting off, searched among them for Cara, but she didn't disembark all the way into town as the bus went down the busy High Street and trundled so agonisingly slowly towards its final destination.

He followed the bus all the way to the depot where it pulled in and the driver turned the engine off. Greg left his car slewed behind the bus at an angle and ran round to the front of it.

'You aren't supposed to drive . here,' the driver said as he got off the bus. 'Buses only! What do you think you're doing?'

'Where is she?' Greg demanded.

'Where's who?'

'You picked up a woman at the hospital. She probably had a suitcase with her.'

'You've lost me, mate. I picked up a lot of people. And dropped them off too. I can't be expected to remember every one of them, but I'm pretty sure none of them had a suitcase.'

Greg shoved past him, stepped up onto the bus and looked down at row upon row of empty seats.

'No!' he shouted.

At the moment Greg was stepping down from the bus and walking back to his car, a taxi pulled up in one of the waiting spaces outside the hospital. Cara, who had been sitting on a bench in the shade, got up and waved to him.

he driver opened his window and
aned out.

'Taxi for the Swan Hotel?'

'That's right,' she murmured. And
when she got back to the hotel she
intended to go straight to bed.

★   ★   ★

Cara turned off the light. She liked the
hotel room. Liked the barren emptiness
of it. This was more like it. This was her
life. Empty. She should have left a note
for Greg, at least thanking him for his
hospitality. He'd tried, after all — they
both had — and look where it had got
them.

She felt bad for just walking out like
that. It had been difficult getting her
case down the stairs, getting dressed,
but she'd managed. She'd proved to
herself that she could manage. She
really didn't need anyone else.

Her mind kept going over the events
of the day, from waking in the morning
to breakfast in bed, to Danny falling in

the pond and then to leaving Greg house for the last time.

She'd left the house with little idea where she was going, and much less where she was. The bus stop at the end of the road had seemed like a good bet and that's where she'd boarded a bus heading for town. She spotted the Swan Hotel from the bus window and pressed the button for the driver to stop.

She had been intending to go straight to the hospital, but she needed to get rid of her suitcase first. She didn't want to look conspicuous at the hospital, didn't want to stand out in any way.

The Swan Hotel was small, set back from the road. It was a bolthole. She booked in under her mother's maiden name just in case anyone — Greg — should try to find her. Once she'd got her breath back, she'd asked the receptionist to call her a taxi to take her to the hospital.

All this went through her mind as she tried to sleep, over and over again. She wondered if she should have done

...ings differently. Waited for Greg to call from the hospital. Waited for him to come home even. Too late now.

She closed her eyes, wished for sleep, but she was awake for a very long time. *What doesn't kill us makes us stronger.* Whoever said that was right. Cara Sanford was going to return home stronger, harder, different. This time the barriers were up and that's where they would stay.

14

Casualties lined the dock while fire officers made the ship safe. Armed police tackled the group of terrorists that had held passengers hostage for several hours and a specialist crew dealt with the dangerous chemical leak, caused by a bomb exploding near the tanker storage area.

The walking wounded queued up and some enterprising soul was serving tea to the emergency services.

Several specialist teams had been launched into action. Off duty doctors, nurses, police officers and firemen had been called in. There had never been so many people on the dock. An emergency field hospital had been set up in the passenger lounge and a photographer from the local press was taking shots of just about everything.

A television crew was there, recording everything as it happened while cheerful casualties displayed their life-threatening injuries to officials.

'I've lost my leg,' one man boasted proudly.

'You think you've got problems,' the guy lying next to him said. 'I've got a hole in my stomach the size of a dinner plate and I'm unlikely to last till the ambulance gets here.'

Greg stood in front of them. 'You could groan a bit,' he chided. 'You know, make it a bit more realistic.'

The men exchanged looks, then both started to howl and moan. Laughing and shaking his head, Greg walked away.

There was an almost carnival atmosphere here. The casualties were enjoying a free day off work and the professionals, like Greg, were revelling in the challenge of getting all these people off the dock and into hospitals and making the dock safe again.

Carter had chosen not to get involved

until he saw the arrival of the television crew. He was being interviewed by the news team now, telling them how this was all his idea. It didn't bother Greg. If Carter wanted to take the credit, it was up to him. He even mustered a smile for him as he walked past.

So far the efforts had been spot-on. Everyone was pulling together and he felt reassured that in the event of a real disaster, they would cope.

The weather was quite different now to how it had been last time Greg was here. An icy November wind snapped in from the sea and there was no sign of any sunshine in the leaden sky. It had been like this for days now; dark skies, icy winds blasting the last of the leaves from the trees and long, cold, frosty nights.

Oh, yes — the nights were so long.

He paused for a moment and looked down the dock. He could almost imagine a slender figure in tight shorts jogging towards him, a radiant smile on her face, hair bobbing.

He wondered where she was now. What she was doing. How she was doing. Was she happy? He hoped she was.

He'd called every hotel in the area and had even called taxi firms asking if anyone had booked to go to the airport.

On the day she should have left, he'd gone to Heathrow airport searching, hoping, but he'd lost her, lost her for good. She could have gone home early. There was no way of knowing. And she hadn't returned to the hospital again to have her bandages tightened.

She'd vanished. Completely and utterly. The only thing he could be sure of was that she was back in Australia now.

'Greg, I have a couple of elderly casualties I'd like you to look at,' Claire called, shaking him out of his thoughts. 'I want them to have priority when it comes to transport to hospital.'

He looked across at two giggling old ladies.

'One of them has had a heart attack and the other one, would you believe, is in a diabetic coma. They're both very ill.'

Gales of laughter rose suddenly from the two old ladies and Greg grinned.

'They're not very good actresses, are they?' he commented. 'Okay, I'm on my way. But I don't hold out much hope of getting them into an ambulance for a while.'

The whole exercise looked like being a resounding success and the fact that Claire was here doing her bit was wonderful, but the dull ache was back in his heart and he didn't know how on earth he was ever going to cure it.

He'd exchanged one heartache for another. They were quite different, but just as destructive, just as painful.

There was one way to end all this. He just wasn't sure he had the courage to do it.

He walked over to the old ladies.

'Okay,' he said. 'Which one of you is the heart attack?'

They both went off into fits of giggles and he couldn't help smiling with them.

* * *

Much later, the quay was almost deserted and there was very little to show for the day's exercise.

Shipping schedules were back on course and the dockers were heading in to start a new shift. The night had closed in and huge spotlights lit up the dock. Icy rain bounced in the beams of light. Everything was back to normal. Life went on.

Greg hung around, reluctant to leave. This was where it all started. And it had ended at his front door.

The last time he'd seen Cara was when he left her at his house, never dreaming she wouldn't be there when he got home. He'd had no idea that he'd never see her again.

He remembered the last time he saw his brother, Brad. It was funny how firsts and lasts stuck so firmly in the mind, he thought. If he'd come home and found Cara waiting that day, he probably would have forgotten those

306

last few moments spent with her, but because they were the last, he'd been over them again and again, seeing her sad, troubled face like a vivid snapshot in his mind.

* * *

It had taken a while, but Cara was back to full fitness. In fact, she was probably fitter than she had been before. She could run further, faster, harder than she could previously and she did so almost every day because when she was running, she didn't have to think. She could let her mind go blank, think only of the ground passing beneath her feet.

Even in this heat, she ran. It had become almost a compulsion, a need, something to fill the empty hours.

When she wasn't running or sleeping, she was working. And they didn't like her much, the people under her in her new department. She'd heard them whispering about her behind her back, saying how she expected everyone to work to her own exacting standards which were virtually impossible for mere mortals to maintain. They said she was rigid, inflexible, heartless. Well, so be it. If that's what they thought, who was she to disappoint them?

Someone who used to work with her years ago now found themselves on her team and she heard them say she'd changed. Yes, she had changed. She'd taken that step into womanhood that changed everyone. But she'd taken it too late and with the wrong person. Or maybe with the right person, but at the wrong time.

Her heart was a stone inside her chest. A cold, hard stone. And she had little heart for the job that had meant so much to her. She gave it her best, she always gave of her best, but she didn't give it her heart.

It was early December and hotter than ever and she wondered what the weather was like in the UK. Much cooler than here, that was for sure. Her calendar, filled with images of Brita. throughout the year, showed a winter landscape, snow whitening the branches of bare trees and blanketing the hills under an impossibly clear blue sky.

She spent as little time as possible in her drab, functional home which sat back from the road. It was an unremarkable, flat white building among other similar flat, white buildings.

And she was almost there, almost at the last corner when she saw the man standing by the kerb on the other side of the road, his jacket slung over his shoulder, a rucksack at his feet. The relentless Australian sunshine gleamed off his almost black hair as he consulted a piece of paper and looked around as if searching for something.

She stopped running and stared at him. There it was again, that violent lurch of her heart. He looked so much like . . . but no, it couldn't be, wasn't possible. Greg was on the other side of the world. He didn't know where to find her. She started to run again, feet ounding the hot pavement.

As she drew closer she saw he wore jeans and an open-necked green shirt which she knew would be almost the same colour as his eyes. He looked up and watched her approach. Tall and lean, his head cocked slightly to one side atop those broad shoulders. It couldn't be — wasn't possible.

She looked away. *Why torture yourself? Why put yourself through it?*

She'd seen him a hundred times since coming home. Imagined him in the crowd at the airport, walking into the hospital, strolling round the park. How many times had she seen a man, felt her heart soar, only to be dragged down with disappointment when she realised it wasn't him? Why should today be any different? She'd conjured him up because she was thinking about the winter weather on the other side of the world. That was all.

If she looked at him again, which she had no intention of doing, she'd probably see his hair was fair, he might have a beard. The only thing that was certain was that he wouldn't be the one person in the world she wanted to see.

Make-up? She hadn't even unpacked it since she got home. It was still in a bag somewhere. What was the point of wearing make-up? The patients weren't bothered. They were sick, hurting, injured — they only cared that she could fix them, take away the pain, make them better. Who was there worth making herself look pretty for?

But now she wished she had some colour on her eyelashes. She wished her vest wasn't clinging so damply to her body and that her hair wasn't quite so scruffy.

She kept her eyes on the pavement directly ahead as she jogged past.

But then he called from the other side of the road.

'Hi.'

'Hi.' Good manners took over and she returned the greeting without thinking, picking up her pace, ready to sprint the last few metres to her home.

Wasn't imagination a wonderful and tormenting thing? It was her imagination that stopped her contacting him. She'd lost count of the letters she'd started to write and the times she'd picked up the phone and got all the way to the end of his number before slamming it down again.

She couldn't bear the thought of making contact and realising that he didn't want to speak to her. Better to let herself believe that she had rejected him than the other way around.

Outside her front door, she reached into her pocket for her key. It was trapped in the deep pocket of her shorts, caught in the thin lining. She didn't normally have this much trouble. It was only a blooming key, for Heaven's sake.

She fumbled, swore, flicked it out of the material at last and her shaking fingers sent it spinning to the ground.

As she turned to pick it up, he was right behind her, already sweeping it up. He looked down at her. This wasn't her imagination. This was real. He was real.

'Do you have any idea how long it's taken me to find you?' he asked.

'I don't know how long you've been looking,' she said breathlessly, but not from running. Her heart was pounding, shaking her whole body, and she wondered if he could hear it.

'All my life. My life since it began again, since I met you. I must have phoned hundreds of hotels, spent hours at the airport in the vain hope of catching a glimpse of you. And then calling the hospitals here until I found where you were, and working out my notice so I could . . . '

'Working your notice?'

He nodded in answer. 'I quit my job. I had to see you . . . '

She stared at him, hardly able to comprehend that he would do this for her.

A sudden dreadful thought gripped her. She'd left without hearing what happened to Danny. What if he'd died?

What if she'd walked out on him at a time of tremendous pain?

'Danny?' she croaked.

'Danny's great,' he said. 'And so's Claire. She's back at the hospital three days a week and Danny's in a fantastic pre-school place. They're both learning to ride as well. How about you? How's the new job?'

'I hate it,' she replied candidly. *Without you, I hate everything, even myself*, she thought to herself.

'Are you healed? You look well.'

Everything but my heart.

'I'm fine.'

'I'm not,' he said. 'I'm not fine without you.'

He stepped forward and wrapped his arms around her, squeezing her tight against him the way he'd wanted to do before, resting his face in her soft hair. She let out a gasp and he released her.

'Am I hurting you?'

'Not any more,' she said, sliding her arms round his waist. 'Hold me, Greg. Hold me tight.'

314

And then she reached up and kissed him. Kissed him as if her life depended on it — and it probably did, for without him she felt sure that eventually she would wither away and die.

He pulled her closer still, moulding her body to his.

He slipped the key into the door and pushed it open, then he swept her up into his arms and carried her over the threshold. The house which had lacked warmth, heart and soul now suddenly hummed with life, with passion.

Still holding her in his arms, he kicked the door shut behind them and kissed her.

'I love you, Cara,' he murmured when they finally came up for air. 'I want to be with you and I don't care where that is, whether it's here or in the UK, or anywhere else in the world.'

'I love you, too, Greg,' she said. 'So very much. And I feel exactly the same. My life is utterly empty without you.'

'Will you marry me, Cara? As soon as we can arrange it?'

'Yes,' she breathed. 'Oh, yes.'

She was ready to give up everything — but it wouldn't really be giving up everything, because Greg was her everything and he always would be.

And whatever the future held for them, wherever the future took them, they would be together. It was where they belonged. Not in any one place, but to each other. Forever.

THE END

We do hope that you have enjoyed reading this large print book.

Did you know that all of our titles are available for purchase?

We publish a wide range of high quality large print books including:
Romances, Mysteries, Classics
General Fiction
Non Fiction and Westerns

Special interest titles available in large print are:
The Little Oxford Dictionary
Music Book, Song Book
Hymn Book, Service Book

Also available from us courtesy of Oxford University Press:
Young Readers' Dictionary
(large print edition)
Young Readers' Thesaurus
(large print edition)

For further information or a free brochure, please contact us at:
Ulverscroft Large Print Books Ltd.,
The Green, Bradgate Road, Anstey,
Leicester, LE7 7FU, England.
Tel: (00 44) 0116 236 4325
Fax: (00 44) 0116 234 0205

SEEK NEW HORIZONS

Teresa Ashby

Sister Dominique, already having serious doubts about her calling, is sent on a mercy mission to South America after a devastating earthquake. There, she meets Dr Steve Daniels, and feelings she had never expected to experience again are stirred up. As she is thrown into caring for a relentless stream of casualties, her thoughts are in turmoil. How will she cope in the outside world if she leaves the sisterhood? And dare she allow herself to fall in love again?

HOUSE OF FEAR

Phyllis Mallett

Jill's twenty-first birthday is more than just a milestone — it marks the day her life changes forever . . . A letter arrives on the morning of her birthday; an invitation to travel to Crag House on the remote Scottish island of Inver to stay with the grandfather whose existence she had been completely unaware of. Whilst there, she meets her cousins, Owen and George, and handsome neighbour Robert Cameron. But her visit has involved her in a web of deceit that may threaten her life . . .

SUSPICIOUS HEART

Susan Udy

When Erin discovers that her mother's home and livelihood is under threat from the disturbingly handsome Sebastian, she knows she has to fight his plans every step of the way. However, she quickly realises Sebastian is equally determined to win, and he apparently has the backing of the entire village. When a campaign of intimidation is begun against Erin and her mother, it doesn't take her long to work out that it can only be Sebastian behind it . . .

THE RUNAWAYS

Patricia Robins

When Judith and Rocky elope to Gretna Green they sincerely believe marriage will solve all their problems. But the elopement proves to be the beginning of an entirely new set of difficulties ... Rocky begins to wonder if his parents were right — is he even in love? Were they too young after all? And in the background Gavin, Judith's boss, watches her disillusionment with a concern which is growing into something more ...

ANGEL'S TEARS

Teresa Ashby

Born in the same year that the Titanic sank, seventeen-year-old Cassandra Grant has the world at her feet. But tragedy strikes her family and Cassie has to grow up fast. She falls in love with Dr Michael Ryan — but then discovers he is about to be engaged to be married. Cassie leaves town to begin training as a midwife and tries to forget Michael, but tragedy strikes again and she has to return home where there are more surprises in store . . .